BA

MAGNUS

VIKING SURRENDER

EMMANUELLE DE MAUPASSANT

Copyright

This is a work of fiction. Names, characters, places, and incidents are either the product of the author's imagination or are used fictitiously. With the exception of well-known historical figures and places, any resemblance to actual persons, living or dead, business establishments, events or locales is entirely coincidental.

Cover Design by Emmy Ellis

ABOUT EMMANUELLE DE MAUPASSANT

Emmanuelle lives with her husband (maker of the best fruit cake ever) and with her little Skye Terrier, Ms. Scruffy, (connoisseur of squeaky toys and bacon treats).
Writing heroines who know their own mind, and heroes who appreciate a woman's worth.

Visit Emmanuelle's website, to sign up for her newsletter: first eyes on new releases, giveaways and gossip.

www.emmanuelledemaupassant.com

Welcome to the Viking Surrender series: a scorchingly hot collection of nine sizzling Viking romances.

If you're yet to read the Prologue to this romance, please do before you dive in to Magnus and Modwen's story.

The Prologue sets the scene for all that happens next, so you don't want to miss out...
(you'll find it available for FREE download from Amazon)

We hope the nine romances in this series provide welcome escape and entertainment, that they inspire you and transport you.

While you're cheering for our heroes and heroines, we want you to cheer for yourself. Like the women and men in these tales, you're stronger than you may realize, more resourceful and more determined.

As for happy endings, we all need to believe that

things can get better if we persevere, that there is hope, and the chance to embrace a life of love and friendship and contentment.

Go get 'em!

VIKING SURRENDER

A horde of battle-hardened, ferocious Nordic warriors.

A Pictish village at the mercy of its enemies.

A harrowing bargain struck for nine fearful and reluctant brides.

Delivered into Viking hands, claimed and conquered, each bride must accept that she belongs to her new master. But, as wedding nights bring surrender to duty, will fierce lovers also surrender their hearts?

The Highland wilderness is savage, life is perilous, and the future uncertain, but each Viking has sworn protection, and there are no lengths to which a man will not go to safeguard the woman he loves.

Nine provocatively sensual tales of suspense, seduction and adventure, told against the forbidding backdrop of medieval Scotland.

Journey together with indomitable heroes and intrepid heroines, as they discover that the raging storms of fear and passion can transform into enduring devotion.

Dare to enter our world

Magnus - by Emmanuelle de Maupassant

Magnus is tortured by memories of his wife's murder at the hands of savage berserkers, yet commanded to wed. The valiant warrior finds unexpected passion in his new bride's arms, but can Modwen's love heal the wounds of his battle-scarred heart—or will another's jealousy destroy them both?

MAGNUS

EMMANUELLE DE MAUPASSANT

1

It had been a good day for sailing.

The wind was whipping her skirts as he kissed her and tugged her long plait. She laughed, returning the caress of his sea-salted lips.

When he returned from fishing with Hagen and Gulbrand, their young sons, she'd have a surprise waiting. Something to serve alongside the fish they'd catch. The lingonberries were ripening, and she knew the best gathering places.

She'd ventured deep into the forest, filling her basket, staining her fingers scarlet. She hadn't known about the attack on Skalanes. Hadn't realised until it was too late.

In his dreams, she didn't scream. Not at first.

Seeing them, she dropped her basket, and the berries spilled.

She ran, but they were swift, those wild-eyed

beast-warriors in predator pelts. Faces dirty above her, they shivered with fevered urge.

Animals—not men. Feasting, until she was broken.

He woke with a jolt.

Solveig!

Gasping for breath, Magnus reached for his axe, his heart racing beneath the terrible, crushing ache in his chest. A wave of nausea followed close on, and he rolled over to retch, heaving until the spasm passed.

There was nothing he could do to bring her back.

His mouth was sour, and he needed to piss, but he kept his eyes closed, resting his fingertips on the sand, willing himself calm.

A third of his lifetime had passed, but still the dreams came—borne of memory and imagination, of what had happened, and his own helplessness to change any of it.

The gods had forsaken him, taking what he most loved, letting her die. Hadn't he lived as Odin would wish? With courage and discipline, self-reliance and honesty?

Wasn't he just and loyal and honourable?

None of that had been enough.

He shifted onto his side, then sat up, looking

out at the glimmering sea. Far, far below, so the *skalds* told them, lay *Jörmungandr*—the great serpent girdling this world, waiting for battle with Thor at the end of days.

All this was to come, ice and fire, death and rebirth from beneath a blackened sun. Eternal. Unstoppable.

And still he breathed, his lungs pulling air in and out, as ceaselessly as the pebbles pushed and drawn by the tide. Blighted and heartless, cast upon this accursed place, and bound by his loyalty to Brandr's command.

To take a wife, of all things.

To bury his misery and embrace this new land.

To put aside his devouring spite and return to what he'd once been.

Impossible.

2

Modwen pushed open one of the great doors that ran across the front of the forge and squinted through the dim interior. There was no reason for them to be closed. The longest days were nigh upon them, and there was yet light in the sky. Plenty to work by.

Two summers had passed since she'd last heard the distinctive ring of hammer upon iron. None in Achnaryrie had the skill nor strength to wield the tools; not since the death of Galan—though their son had been soon to begin learning his father's trade.

The sound carried across their jutting peninsula, high above the sea. Perhaps even down the cliff path to the beach, where the rest of the Norsemen were encamped.

Having feasted well, they were mostly sleeping, sated with drink and food, but the man she must now call husband was here. With only the illumination of the furnace to guide him, he struck at the clasps of the shackles he'd been set to mending.

Shackles for Rhiannon.

Foolhardy of the girl to have drawn her dagger. More foolish still to have wounded one of these strangers, the brother of their jarl, no less. If he died, she'd pay dearly.

Reckless and misguided, but admirable, too, Rhiannon had never given up the will to fight, taking up arms to defend against those who would plunder.

From the south and west, beyond the forests and the fast-flowing waters of Dunnock Burn, had come raiders—first to trade, but then to steal. Through skirmishes and constant fighting, Achnaryrie had become a settlement of women, its menfolk killed or harshly wounded.

Many nights, Modwen had lain awake, wondering what would become of them. Few livestock remained, and they'd scarce had strength to plant this year's crops.

Their chieftain, Domnall, reclined upon his sickbed, little able to bargain on their behalf.

The arrival of these Norsemen was a blessing. Some might call the marriages to which they'd consented no better than servitude, but what choice did they have? To resist and be enslaved?

Better to make a truce, as Eithne had bartered for them.

"I've ale for you, husband—and food." She held out the richly fragranced trencher, well-piled with roasted boar. It had been months since her people had eaten so well. Not only fierce warriors, the Norsemen they'd invited within their walls were good huntsmen, too.

He knew she was here, surely, but made no reply, keeping his head bent to the anvil. Again, Magnus lifted the hammer, a single spark flying as its weight connected with the metal below. What would he look like in battle, she wondered, using those powerful warrior arms to wield an axe or sword?

Gathering her courage, Modwen moved closer.

With her eyes growing accustomed to the dark, she saw he'd thrown off his leather tunic and was stripped bare to the waist.

His skin glistened with sweat—from the heat of the flames and exertion. How powerful his arms were, the muscles flexing with each raising of the hammer. She took in the breadth of his chest and great shoulders, the strength of his neck and jaw. A strange pattern covered his abdomen—eight arrows, forked, radiating from the centre. Another adorned his right arm—like the handle of a sword. She frowned. No, a hammer, of course, interwoven with knots.

A thick scar bisected his left eyebrow, passing jagged through his cheek. Others, smaller, marred the sun-darkened skin of his chest and shoulders. A single, curving wound had sliced his rigid abdomen.

He was a stranger to her, but something primitive within herself responded to the sight of him. She knew that feeling. That hunger.

She hadn't forgotten Galan, but he was no longer here to claim her, to protect or comfort her. She belonged to this man now, and his pleasure would be her bidding. If she were fortunate, he'd be considerate and gentle—he'd uphold the vows he'd made before Father Godfrey, keeping her and the children safe and well-fed.

Had he been waiting for her all this time? Expecting her to come? Was he angry that she'd not presented herself sooner?

If so, then to show herself willing would be wise. There was no soft place to lay in the forge, but men seemed to care little for such comfort.

Alpia and Taran were safely abed in the hut.

Placing the victuals and ale upon the bench of tools, Modwen took another step. Swiftly, she unlaced the fastening at the front of her gown to reveal the softer fabric of her smock beneath.

All through the day, she'd been aware of what must come. Had thought of little else, if truth be told, but how his body would feel, pressed upon hers.

Now the moment was at hand, a sudden fear gripped her. She knew nothing of her new husband's tastes.

Galan had never hurt her; at least, not intentionally. What of this Magnus? He had the strength to make her submit to whatever stirred him.

His hammer had fallen still, but his eyes remained downcast, and he appeared to frown.

For what did he wait? Her supplication?

Should she discard both garments, to stand naked before him? Her body was his more than her own, so the sacrament of marriage dictated, but she rebelled at presenting herself so. Didn't she deserve some token of courtship, despite the circumstances of their joining?

Perhaps his ways were different. Or, had she disappointed him? She was younger than he, but ten summers older than most of the other women. Did he think her unworthy?

She'd birthed two babes, and her body was yet strong.

Heated by indignation, she pulled down the yoke of her smock, baring her breasts. Let him see for himself.

She was no willow branch, her womanhood as lush as any man could desire. If he doubted it, let him test the firmness of her flesh.

"Husband?" She sought to muster some defiance, to let him see that she wouldn't be ignored but, when he raised his head, her breath caught.

His eyes bore no trace of warmth, nor feeling. With lips pressed tight, he was all aversion, as if her presence were vile to him.

She knew not whether to cover herself and flee, or to fall upon her knees in entreaty.

A shiver passed through her as she stood, exposed under his hateful gaze.

Could she not see that he'd no stomach for meat nor ale? He'd removed himself to escape the mirth of those who would celebrate this day, and to escape the sight of her!

The *skækja* was brazen, showing him the goods of purchase.

She was comely enough, but he was in no mood to consummate this sham of a marriage.

In fealty to Brandr, he'd fulfilled his obligation, speaking the necessary vows. Yet, they'd stuck in his throat.

He'd grown from child to man alongside Brandr, and his loyalty sprung from friendship as much as duty. His Solveig had been cousin to Brandr's wife, Sigrunn—lost the year before in delivering his child.

What deception had Brandr's new bride worked to entice their jarl into this pact? Some enchantment was afoot, for the other men from Skalanes seemed far too willing to take these Pictish wenches to wife.

He'd have none of it.

It was doubtful the gods blessed these pairings,

for what rituals had been observed? They'd offered their sacrificial blót, but none of the boar's blood had been sprinkled upon them, and they'd given no exchange of ancestral swords.

As to the bridal ale, Brandr had been obliged to use their own store from the ships, Achnaryrie having exhausted its own supply of honeyed mead.

Magnus remembered, still, the night before his wedding to Solveig, going to the bath house to purify himself for the ceremony. Her father had made clear what he expected, laying out Magnus's duties as husband. How proud he'd been, to take Solveig from the older man's protection.

His bride had never looked more beautiful, in her crown of straw and wheat garlanded with cornflowers, her golden plaits looped between the blooms. And how brightly her eyes had shone.

Magnus grimaced.

Her father, at least, had not lived to see the cruel destiny woven for her.

At Brandr's wish, in Achnaryrie he would stay, keeping weapons sharp and the farming tools in good order. No man would accuse him of failing his duty, but his time of husbanding was over. That, he'd leave to younger men.

Meanwhile, he wished to be left with the hammer and the flames, shaping iron to his will.

The wench yet brandished herself for his appraisal.

"Be gone," he growled.

To his annoyance, she didn't move, though her eyes grew wide, and he detected the first sheen of coming tears. She trembled under his glare.

Angered, he flung the hammer away, sending it thudding across the earthen floor. He clenched his fists. If need be, he'd throw her physically from his place of refuge.

"Be gone, woman!"

This time, his tone could not be mistaken.

With a cry of dismay, she clasped together the fabric of her gown and, clutching it to her, ran from his sight.

3

Spring had been late coming but had lifted the mist with zeal that morning. Savouring the warmth of the sun on her back, Modwen stood at her loom, with Alpia beside her.

"Like this, remember?" Carefully, Modwen adjusted the heddle to separate the warp threads.

Alpia took the shuttle in her hand, passing it through to the end of the row.

"Don't forget to use the beater." Modwen brought it down with a gentle tap. "It keeps the weft even and makes the cloth strong and beautiful."

Alpia nodded, giving the task her concentration.

Modwen kissed the top of her daughter's head. How quickly she was growing up.

The girl had been frightened by the arrival of the Norsemen, as they all had, but seemed now to be more at ease. Last night, she'd even served ale to the warriors, moving deftly from one to the next without spilling anything from her jug. Modwen hadn't liked the idea, but no harm had come. The men had been boisterous but had kept the bawdiest of their behaviour for their brides.

Except Magnus, of course. As soon as their vows had been spoken, and the boar's throat cut, he'd removed to the forge. The evening hadn't gone as she'd thought it might. He'd wanted nothing to do with her.

Little wonder, perhaps. They were strangers, after all.

But--still--she'd expected him to take what was freely offered. Most men would have. Instead, he'd appeared angry, though she couldn't think why. He seemed not to understand her, and she knew none of his language, so it couldn't have been anything she'd said.

Ridiculous man!

He'd slept on the forge's hard floor, she supposed.

Before dawn, she'd heard the Norsemen setting off to fulfil the first part of their bargain to Achnaryrie.

'Twill be a sorry day for the Nechtain, and for Eanfrith's band of cutthroats! The thought came to her almost gleefully, before Modwen chided herself. A good Christian woman shouldn't delight in the deaths of her enemies, even though they deserved it.

A sudden yelp focused her attention.

Outside Brigid's hut, Taran was playing with Bram. The two boys were sparring with their wooden swords, inspired, no doubt, by the warriors who walked among them. Though Taran was taller, Bram had caught him under the ribs with the point of his little weapon.

"Be careful!"

Taran turned at Modwen's warning but merely grinned.

"I'm not hurt, Mother! We're practising our fighting skills. I want to show Jerrik, Alarik, and Steinn when they return."

He wasn't afraid at least, of these warriors who now held sway. Taran hadn't mentioned Magnus, though. In truth, they'd hardly met. Modwen sighed. All things would come in time.

She glanced towards the other end of the village, at the forest.

Will he come back?

Of course he would.

From the other end of the row of huts, Eithne was approaching.

Her father-in-law near death and her late husband's sister in shackles, yet how calm she seems. Modwen frowned. It had been Eithne's idea to make these marriage contracts. No doubt she was pleased. Wasn't everything just as she'd hoped?

Some of the Norsemen were to be sent to trade for grain, she'd heard, and there were plans to till the fields above the clifftops, making them ready for sowing. Already, work was underway. When the time came, Taran and Alpia could do their part, picking stones from the turned soil.

"Such a lovely colour."

She jumped at Eithne's voice. Modwen's cheeks grew hot, but she inclined her head in recognition of the compliment.

"Bitter vetch and wild cress for the dye. They give a deep violet, and I use saltwater for the fixing."

Modwen was proud of her knowledge. None other in Achnaryrie knew how to bring such vivid colours to wool nor wove their cloth so well. Even through these hard months, she'd been able to trade her weaving for provisions.

In return for warm blankets and good cloth for a cloak, Ytha had brought rabbit for her pot all through winter. Modwen wondered how the girl was faring with her husband. A hulking brute, like all the rest. She'd looked for Ytha in vain at the feast.

The girl spent most of her time in the forest and did none any harm, though there was something about her eyes. There were rumours, too, of her being cursed. The year she'd been born, the crops had failed. Modwen had been only a child at the time, yet she remembered something of it. Many in the village were wary of Ytha, but in truth, she was a gentle soul.

Eithne was stroking the cloth upon the loom. "The shade will suit you. Your husband will think you well in it."

Modwen lowered her eyes. It was too shaming to admit that her Norseman found no pleasure in her. She'd worn her finest gown, of golden hue, for their marriage vows, the dye ground from cow weed and bracken roots.

He'd barely glanced at her.

As for his surly behaviour later that night, Modwen was humiliated to think on it.

Meanwhile, it was evident that her friend was well content in her own match. The jarl had made no bones in choosing fair Eithne, and Modwen had noticed them soon slipping away to the privacy of their hut. As fierce as Brandr was, he must know how to please his bride, for Eithne was filled with serene radiance.

Modwen pressed her lips closed, wishing to say nothing rather than betray her envy.

It seemed that all Achnaryrie was taking advantage of the fine weather. Others had come to sit outside, bringing their chores into the sunshine, mending clothes and peeling vegetables. Three of the older women squinted at Modwen and Eithne--curious, she supposed. They were different now, wedded as they were to these Norsemen.

Someone else was watching, too, from an open doorway. Modwen averted her gaze, having no wish to encourage him, but those eyes were not easily deterred.

With his customary scowl, Fecir was approaching.

Modwen swallowed and endeavoured to keep her expression neutral, but Eithne must have noticed her discomfort, for she looked fleetingly over her shoulder. Seeing who approached, she gave an apologetic half-smile.

"I must get on." Eithne touched Modwen's arm. "Feidelm will want to see me."

No sooner had she departed than Fecir sidled up, his face soured and sneering. She knew his shoulder pained him--a wound sustained shortly after Galan's death, and which had left him unable to raise his right arm--but he'd worn the same grimace even before.

As her late husband's uncle, he'd once spent much time in their home and had provided another pair of hands in the forge. But since her widowhood, Modwen had done her utmost to withdraw. Fecir had always been too familiar, finding ways to touch her that were unwelcome.

In recent months, he'd made little effort to disguise his lewd suggestions. He'd even gone behind her back, pressing Domnall to agree that a wedding between them would be wise--that the children would benefit from his protection. Thank the heavens, Feidelm had intervened, urging that Modwen needed more time to grieve.

Fecir brought his face close to Modwen's, so close that his spittle landed upon her cheek.

"Found someone good enough, have we?" His fingers clasped her forearm. "Someone you'll open your legs for?"

Modwen flinched and glanced at Alpia. "Let's put aside our weaving for a while." She forced herself to smile. "Fetch water from the stream and get your brother to help you. When Magnus returns, he'll want to bathe. I've set the largest pot over the fire. Fill it to near the brim."

Fecir's long nails dug through her sleeve. Modwen swallowed a cry of pain, not wanting him to know how much he was hurting her.

"Was it rough?" His mouth curved in a leer. "I've heard they like it rough."

"He's my husband, and it's no business of yours." She tried to wrench away, aiming a kick at Fecir's shin, but his grip only tightened.

Modwen's eyes prickled with tears.

"My forge, though, isn't it? Been in my family all these years." He spat on the ground. "That filth has no right to come here taking what's mine."

"It's still in your family!" Modwen protested. "Taran needs to learn."

In one swift motion, she brought down her heel upon Fecir's toes. Then, as he loosened his hold, she jabbed her elbow into his face. With a yelp, he raised his hands, cursing her.

Modwen's heart raced. Never before had she

dared stand up to him. She was glad of it. Exhilarated! She should have done so long ago. But her stomach churned as hatred burned in his eyes. He wiped his wrist beneath his nose, leaving a smear of blood across his cheek.

He clenched his left hand, and Modwen waited for him to strike her, but he seemed suddenly to think better of it.

"I won't forget." He glanced at the group of older women, staring at them across the way, then hissed his parting words. "Fair is fair, wench, and I'll have what's mine."

4

If he lived, it would be for Odin to decide, for the Valkyries would weave crimson slaughter on their loom this day.

With a cold heart, he'd fight, and his armour would be *Aegishjalmr,* the Helm of Awe, inked upon his stomach, and *Mjölnir*—Thor's own hammer—etched upon his arm. His back needed no chainmail nor reindeer hide for protection, for there was placed Odin's own spear—*Gungnir*. These were his cloak, and he had no need for another.

He took neither helmet nor shield, all the better to wield his weapons dual-handed. Like the dragon, Fafnir, he would wreak havoc on the sons of men, and all who beheld the symbols would cower, knowing the wrath of the true gods before they met the bite of his blade.

The mighty ones of Valhalla had allowed Solveig to die, but he would honour them yet, showing he feared naught, to earn his place in the golden halls of the gods.

Before dawn's breaking, they moved with stealth through the forest's great oaks, birch, and pine. How hushed it was, their footsteps soft upon velvet moss and long-sodden leaves, as if they were quite alone in the silent dark. Only now and then came the faint rustle of small creatures moving. If wolf or deer abided near, they kept their peace as the Norsemen passed.

They emerged into mist upon fair meadows which marked the Nechtain tribe's land, and found no one on watch, the settlement sleeping, unprotected. In a small pen, goats jostled, bleating quietly.

The warriors of Skalanes drew their swords—Death-maker, Blood-hungry, Viper, and Wolf-fang. Magnus unsheathed *Banamaðr*—Slayer—from its scabbard. Forged from layers of steel in great heat, it was the equal of any.

Together they would fight, each keen for the triumph of the kill, yet guarding the backs of those alongside. In this they were united, for no man battled alone, and the victory would serve them all.

Quickly, they ranged from home to home, preparing for Brandr's signal to attack, the jarl himself taking the largest dwelling. There, the chieftain must reside. With Olav and Magnus flanking him, Brandr found the door unbarred, though two guards dozed inside. Without hesitation, the Norsemen slit their throats.

Finding the leader of their enemy snoring beneath a bed of furs, they dispatched him with similar ease, the only sound from his throat a strangled gurgle, the blood rising to his lips, and his eyes frozen in horror. His wife and three daughters they left unharmed to sob over his corpse.

With Nechtain's men caught unwary, the warriors' task was swift. Few had chance to grasp a weapon before they were brought low. Some stood their ground, fighting as they believed they must, to defend those who quailed inside. Even the strongest proved little contest for the superior might of their foe. Their life streamed scarlet, hot to the soil.

Knowing they were beaten, some threw down their arms. Others fled, leaving their women and children.

Standing in the midst of that crimson scene, there came to Magnus the image of another time and place. Skalanes, on that fateful day—his own people caught unawares. And Solveig, who should have been safe in the forest...

With axe drawn, Magnus took aim at a man some fifty paces off, running to save his own hide. He sent his weapon flying, tumbling head over grip to its target, landing with a thud that split the coward's skull in two.

The trial was over almost before it had begun,

and those men of Nechtain who yet breathed, were brought to kneel upon the ground, to hear their fate.

"No more will you trespass on those lands beyond the forest, unless it be to trade in peace or to deliver what you owe."

Brandr nodded to Olav and Thorolf, sending them to count the livestock penned and assess the stores.

He looked long and hard at each wretch bent before him, and at the women and elderly who stood to one side, though none had the mettle to raise their gaze to meet his. The children he'd sent to wait in the chieftain's hall, for 'twas better for them not to see what was to come.

"There will be mercy for the old and the very young, and for your women," spoke Brandr. "But the men of Nechtain must answer for the menacing of Achnaryrie, and a forfeit will be taken."

Following his jarl's command, Magnus placed a log before the first, and Ragnar held the man's right hand steady, his fingers laid vulnerable. The man raised his head, eyes wild with dread, attempting to struggle to his feet.

Ragnar was obliged to cudgel him above the brow and, with blood dripping down his cheek, the man was stilled.

Magnus made no delay in delivering the blade of his axe.

The captive met the severance of his fingers

with a ghastly scream and rolled back upon the ground, clutching the stumps to his chest, cut cleanly above the second knuckle.

At this, the other men pleaded and made attempt to rise, but Garth, Alarik, and Jerrik were fast behind, pushing them back to their knees.

One to the next, Magnus moved, his axe imparting the same portion, until the deed was done.

Brandr's voice was firm. "Of all you have, we expect you to deliver half to Achnaryrie on the morrow, and think us merciful that we leave you what remains."

It took some hours to locate Eanfrith's camp. The sun was low in the sky before smoke rose in the distance and they smelt meat roasting. Just south of the forest, close upon the flow of Dunnock Burn, the company numbered near thirty men.

Skirting through the shadow of the trees, ten of the warriors formed a line, preparing their spears—each as tall as a man and half yet again. The weapon's iron point was sharp enough to pierce a man through. They were Magnus's own handiwork, each arrow and spearhead crafted in his forge.

The rest of Brandr's warriors separated off, moving low through the long grass of the meadow to surround the other sides of the bandit camp.

"Live by the sword, die by the spear," joked Alarik, surveying the unsuspecting men. "And quickly, I hope, for my stomach's eager for a leg of whatever cooks over yonder fire."

Jerrik and Steinn chuckled their assent, but Brandr hushed them.

"Swift and sure, men of Skalanes! There will be time enough for feeding afterwards."

At the drop of his arm, they let fly their spears, and all but five met their mark, lodging through ribs and shoulders, one splitting a man clean through the neck.

With fury, the others rose, and the true savagery of the day began.

Bellowing his war cry, Magnus plunged into the melee, hacking on all sides. With a double thrust of sword and dagger, he slit the belly of one man and skewered another through the throat. A figure of eight with his sword severed a man's hand from his arm. His fellow Vikings were at his back, but Magnus fought as if he would take on all alone, slashing left and right. If Eanfrith himself were among the slain, Magnus knew not. Each man was the same—a foe to be slaughtered, without pity.

He roared in triumph, revelling in the power coursing through him, to bring pain and darkness and death. He became each man he killed, wearing their blood on his skin, the divide between life and death shimmering on the edge of his vision, a flickering shadow.

At last, there was none standing to receive the bite of his sword, but one was yet alive, crawling through the long grass, dragging himself, bloodied and broken.

Raising Slayer, Magnus drove the point of the blade into the base of the man's skull. A quick end.

He wiped the sweat from his face and joined the others.

The roasting meat was a young sow. Magnus carved a slice from the belly and brought it to his lips. Hot and greasy, it was delicious.

Despite all, the gods had no wish for him in Valhalla.

Not yet.

"Good to see you returned to your old self." Brandr grinned, looking over at Magnus. "Thor's own furnace has been boiling your blood."

Olav slapped Magnus's back. "Aye! But, he'll be catching his death from that bare-chest, now the battle's done."

"Not Magnus!" Alarik declared, locking his elbow round Magnus's neck. "He has a nice warm *víf* warming the bed. That's what's keeping his fire burning."

"Aye! And mine!" Steinn grasped the front of his trousers with a lewd gesture. "I've a *kvenna* of my own waiting, making my loins grow hot."

There was much laughter at that and a few

choice comments on the assets of the new brides of Achnaryrie.

Magnus shrugged off Alarik's playful wrestling and held his peace. If they wanted to think him content, he'd say naught to change that. His woes were not those of other men, and there was no reason for them to bear his burden.

"Salvage as much as you can," Brandr directed. "Swords, daggers—whatever you can find. We'll have need of the metal, if not of the weapons themselves. We'll keep Magnus's forge busy with these pickings. Be quick about it, for 'twill be easier to find our way back through the forest with some daylight to guide us."

Having bent to their task, Brandr came to walk alongside Magnus as they headed across the open field, returning to the forest's edge. "I know your mind, old friend."

He rested his hand on Magnus's arm. "There's opportunity for a new life here. Eleven years is a long time."

Magnus didn't trust himself to speak but kept his step even with his jarl. Brandr, at least, had some notion of his grief, having lost Sigrunn. It was not the same, of course.

Not like what had happened to Solveig.

Nothing compared to that.

Three other women had been killed that day, by the savages who'd swept into Skalanes, intent on plunder. But they had all been elderly, and widows.

They'd left sons and daughters to wail their sorrow, but not husbands.

"A man can become too lost in remorse, unable to look past what might have been."

Magnus raised his eyes to meet those of Brandr.

"I believe in our future here, kinsman. 'Tis long past the day when we should bury ourselves in regret." Brandr gave Magnus a pensive smile. "To see you regain some measure of good cheer will fill my heart, as I know my happiness shall lift yours."

Magnus's throat grew tight, and he merely nodded.

They'd entered the shelter of the pines once more, the dappled shade turning the air cooler.

Brandr paused, his face intent.

"Hear you that, friend?" He looked through the trees. "A snapping of twigs, as of some creature's tread. A stag, mayhap." He reached for his bow, slung upon his back, and raised his hand to still the chatter of the men behind them.

Magnus strained his ear but heard nothing, save for his own breath and the distant call of some roosting bird.

Brandr fitted his arrow and took several steps into the ferns, until he reached a broad oak. There, he stopped, peering through the gloom.

The next moment, he gave a mournful cry. There was a flash of movement from behind the tree—a figure running, pushing through the dense growth—and the jarl let fly his arrow, striking his target clean through the neck.

Brandr turned and staggered. His eyes were disbelieving. Falling to the ground, he clutched at the dagger's hilt protruding from his ribs, buried deep.

Magnus leapt to his jarl's side. He knew not what to do. The dagger must stay or he'd bleed to death before they got him back home.

"One of Eanfrith's men." Brandr gasped, his hand clasped to his wound. "Hiding." He winced, biting his lip against the pain, then groaned and coughed, the spittle on his lip dark with blood.

"Don't speak, my jarl," said Garth, quickly joining Magnus. "You slayed him. Now, breathe shallow and try not to move."

Ragnar and Thorolf, having set off in pursuit, soon returned.

"The cur must have been emptying his bowels when he heard our attack," Ragnar growled. "We'd never have known he was there if Brandr hadn't struck upon him. By Odin, 'tis the worst of luck!"

"So it is," Jerrik answered, "but the gods shall not fail us. There is still light enough to see, and this path's well-trodden."

Making haste, they bore up their jarl, six men taking his weight, moving as swiftly as they could without disturbing Brandr's comfort, taking turns in their burden, to maintain their pace.

Will he die? Magnus sickened at the thought.

First Bjorn and now Brandr. Both injured unto death. If the dagger had pierced Brandr's lung, his life would hang in the balance.

Magnus shifted his friend's weight upon his shoulder. He would carry him the whole way without complaint, though, suddenly, his fatigue was bone-deep.

Were the gods punishing him? If so, for what? A surfeit of pride, or not enough? For wasting his life, or having revelled in too much joy, in the arms of his Solveig?

For more than ten years, he'd let them raid without him. Some men had to remain, he'd argued, to protect Skalanes. Only Brandr's insistence had made him come—and look what had happened.

I am cursed, bringing death to those I care for. They should have left me behind.

5

Modwen paced the forge, lighting the wick of her dish of oil and testing the temperature of the water in the wooden tub. Though it was still warm, she'd fetch another pail from the pot heating over the fire.

For some hours, she'd remained alert for the Norsemen's return. The moon had risen bright, but might they have become lost on the forest path? She didn't wish to dwell on other causes of delay.

Most of the residents of Achnaryrie sat around the fire, waiting, but Modwen had put the children to bed and walked to the edge of the forest. She stared intently down the path, willing to see some sign of their approach—as if her presence would be enough to summon them. To summon him. Magnus.

Strangely, Graeme had been lingering, whittling

something from a piece of wood. He'd scowled on seeing her, making it clear he sought no company.

Perhaps mine isn't the only marriage yet to be consummated, Modwen thought wryly.

His new wife was the jarl's sister, she recalled—and fearsome. Another like their own Rhiannon, with warrior blood in her veins. Graeme would have his hands full there.

Everyone has their worries. Modwen sighed. She'd do best to concentrate on her own.

Tipping in the extra water, she wondered if her preparation would find favour with her husband. Perhaps, he wouldn't send her away this time. She had a jug of ale ready for him, some cold pork, and a bannock.

I shall make a good wife.

And then we'll see what kind of husband he can be...

Once more, she went to the doors of the forge. From far off, she thought she heard something. A whistle? And then a shout?

Yes. Voices.

Then, she saw them. The men.

They'd been carrying someone but had laid him down, two of their number helping him to stand, supporting him on either side.

Who was it? Modwen's stomach clenched.

Let it not be him.

Others had heard them, too. Rinda ran past, and Eithne.

From among the crowd, one stepped forward,

staggering a little. As he came closer, the distinctive scar through his left eyebrow became clear.

"Dear God!" Modwen's hands flew to her mouth.

He was crimson-spattered, his face streaked with blood.

He met her eye briefly, then pushed open the forge doors. With sagging shoulders, he unclasped his belt, letting drop the weapons he was carrying.

The ale he took greedily, downing the cup in a single, gulping draft, then twisted to remove his leather cuff, stained dark. His jaw tightened; Modwen motioned to aid him, and he nodded.

Her fingers shook, unfastening the buckles. Scanning his body, she fought a wave of dizziness. How much of the blood was his own?

She crouched upon the floor to unlace the leather thongs securing the skins about his feet and lower legs. His trousers he saw to himself, groaning as he bent forward.

Her breath caught to look at him.

Solidly muscled, his stomach was smooth and firm. His legs were thick as tree trunks, and what lay between matched the rest of him, girthed as boldly as her wrist.

He lurched forward with a grunt, and she swallowed hard.

Did he intend to take her now, smeared in blood and sweat?

Then, she saw that he meant to climb into the

wooden tub she'd readied. Lowering himself, he exhaled, easing back to dunk his head, letting the water flow over his hair and face. He rubbed to wipe away the grime before emerging again to shake his long, dark mane, leaving tendrils hanging damp. He smoothed back his hair and, with eyes closed, rested his nape upon the rim.

His chest, so wide it filled the breadth of the tub, bore a purple welt. Though the skin seemed unbroken, a dark smear remained on his collarbone—blood, and thicker matter. She shuddered.

She didn't wish to think on it, but she did wish to bathe him.

It was a wife's duty to care for her husband—to feed his belly, provide clean clothes to warm him, and see to his physical ease.

Wearied and bruised, he needed her comfort. He'd risked his life, hadn't he, for the sake of Achnaryrie? To bring them peace and the chance of a future.

His future, too, of course, and that of his fellow Norsemen.

She dipped a square of cloth into the water and drew it gently down his arm, taking the linen across his palm before pressing between his fingers.

Thankfully, he appeared unhurt, but for his bruises. Nevertheless, he lay still, giving no indication of pleasure at her touch.

Wetting the cloth again, she laid it upon his

chest. He flinched slightly, half opening his eyes. She passed the linen over his damp curls, feeling for the hard rim of each nipple.

In response, he drew back his lips from his teeth, as if he wished for her to leave him be, though he said nothing.

I won't go, she thought vehemently.

Surveying his abdomen, she perused the wheel of forks. Did all these Norsemen have the same? She drew downwards, her hands slick upon his wet skin, wishing to touch the strange design.

He moaned, and she drew back. His whole body seemed to tense. Mayhap, there was some injury beneath the skin. Even his hands were clenched as he turned his head, his jaw set.

If her touch caused pain, she would cease, but she wished to ease the memories of the day, which surely troubled him.

Of course, there was one thing that would relax him as nothing else, if he would but allow her.

His knees, resting to either side, afforded her a view of what she'd admired before, now standing proud from his dark thatch.

Modwen moved lower, tracing the line of hair that led to his manhood. She glanced up, and found his gaze fixed now upon her, his eyes bright in the dimly lit room.

A strange flutter travelled through her stomach as he brought his hand over hers.

Firmly, he guided her to his thickness, closing

his fist around her fingers so that she wrapped his shaft.

How strange it was, to be touching him. Not the man she'd married all those years ago, and to whom she'd borne children, but a stranger. A new husband, whose body she must learn.

Guiding her, he began a steady rhythm, back and forth. Raising his hips slightly, he squeezed on the upward stroke, relaxing his pressure on the down. The movement brought forth his slickness.

Placing her dark plait over one shoulder, she leant forward. Despite his bath, he smelt of sweat and earth—and arousal.

Modwen licked her lips.

She wished to taste him.

The trembling that had begun in her belly moved lower, forming a heated ache between her legs.

She belonged to him, but in this act, he would be hers.

She extended her tongue to the glossy bead, sampling his brine, then opened fully, giving him the warmth of her mouth.

He inhaled sharply as she devoured him and swelled further within her hand. She drew downwards, slowly, relishing his length, caressing his engorgement.

She took him deeper, and he groaned and cursed.

Her balance was precarious, and the position

not one of comfort, but the desire to possess this part of him pushed all other thoughts from her mind.

The pressure of his hand lifted, and she plunged her own beneath the water, reaching under to seize the source of his seed. Humming against his hardness, she worked him with her mouth until he held her head, making her still.

With a deep-throated growl, he jerked and pulsed, sending his offering into her throat.

Her heart leapt.

He will be mine.

6

Magnus drew the whetstone across his weapon's edge and tested the blade with his thumb. Sharp enough to slice the skin if he applied but a little more pressure.

He moved farther into the light, holding the sword straight to view its length. With the small marks of battle polished out, it shone brightly again.

His Slayer. Double-edged and inlaid with gold, it was a testament to its maker's skill. His grandfather had beaten the precious metal into chiselled grooves before welding in the heat of the fire. The runes read: No man shall escape *Banamaðr.*

The other side bore the Valknut—three interlocking triangles to represent the nine worlds, and Odin's power of life over death. The pommel and hilt, perfectly weighted to balance the blade, were the finest steel.

Magnus had learnt his trade as men in his family had done for generations. He'd taught his own sons, and they'd made him proud, crafting weapons sought by the finest warriors.

Back in the forge, in Skalanes, were they thinking of him, Hagen and Gulbrand?

Probably not. Both had taken wives not long ago. There was one child born, and another on the way. Their lives were just beginning, and their work was busy.

Would he see them again?

His throat grew tight.

Perhaps.

He lowered *Banamaðr* and sheathed it.

The metal and the heat were all he needed.

Achnaryrie's forge was almost as well-appointed as his own. The fire pit was substantial and the space large enough to move about easily. The light was good, too, one side of the building facing south and able to open entirely, thanks to two sets of heavy doors.

Brandr had made himself clear: 'Achnaryrie needs a forge.'

He promised prosperity for all who stayed.

Good luck to them, Magnus had thought.

It was an opportunity most had seized eagerly, land being in short supply back in Skalanes—and each man had the right to choose his own path.

Except that Brandr hadn't given Magnus a choice.

He hadn't intended to stay, and he'd certainly had no desire to take another wife, but reviving the forge meant commitment to the old smith's widow and his children.

Modwen.

He rubbed at his beard and frowned.

He'd intended to keep his distance, sleeping and eating in the forge.

After he'd lost Solveig all those years ago, everyone had urged him to marry again, saying it would heal his grief.

The thought had been abhorrent. Instead, he'd purchased thralls to keep the house, watch over his sons, and meet his other needs.

But he'd found no real satisfaction in having sex with a woman for whom he felt nothing—a woman he merely owned, and who'd been owned by another before him.

It had given him some relief, but he'd been unable to stop thinking of Solveig. Of her lips on his abdomen and her gentle fingers. Her voice murmuring his name as he'd pleasured her pliant body.

Bedding both thralls at the same time had made the act easier. He hadn't then compared it with what he'd shared with Solveig. It was just fucking. But even that had left him with a deep-seated wretchedness, and it had been years since he'd had the appetite to bring a woman to his bed.

What had he been thinking on the night they'd

returned from the attack upon Eanfrith's bastards, and those other wretches?

When Modwen had bathed him, he'd tried to pay no mind, but the wench's touch was too much for him to ignore.

He'd forgotten how good it could feel—a woman's hand, and a woman's mouth. His cock stirred at the remembrance, but it made no difference.

Allowing himself that intimacy had been a mistake, and one he didn't plan to repeat.

Modwen was not unappealing. Far from it, with her lustrous hair and the curves a woman gained after bearing children. And her eyes—dark green like churning, stormy seas. Eyes to drown a man, if he were of another mind, but that part of his life was in the past.

Solveig had been all the wife he'd ever wanted, and no other would take her place.

He would provide for Modwen and the children, as was his duty.

No more.

7

Modwen stood at her bench, cutting vegetables to add to yesterday's broth. Turning over a turnip, she sighed and plunged to its centre.

So much had changed.

Achnaryrie had regained its stolen livestock, and more besides. An ox now pulled the plough, and the separate plots for each family were gone, replaced by shared land for farming. Alpia and Taran viewed it all as a game, taking their turns to plant and weed, or bringing victuals to the working men.

With four of Achnaryrie's fishing boats repaired, the Norsemen had been landing a good catch. Taran had gone out with them, though only to the edge of the bay. Brigid's boy, Bram, had almost drowned not long ago and, though Taran was a strong swimmer, Modwen was anxious at the thought of him falling overboard. However, all had been well, and their methods of netting fish had certainly proven effective. The smokehouse hung full of mackerel and trout.

The Norsemen's leader, Brandr, seemed likely to live, and with his brother also recovering, perhaps they'd return Rhiannon her freedom.

Modwen had been watching the other women closely, Brigid, Ailsa, Ytha, Myrna, and Eithne. All seemed content, even Gladys!

It hadn't escaped Modwen's notice how often doors were closed in the middle of the day, wives escorted inside, to appear later with flushed cheeks.

She'd joined the others in learning the language of the Norse, tutored each morning by Alarik. He had a wife waiting for him, she'd heard. A lucky woman, for he was of lively humour and had more gentleness in him than most.

The changes appeared all for the good, and Modwen knew she should be happy. Why then did she wake each morning with a strange ache in her heart?

She could not be wholly loathsome to this new husband of hers, yet almost a week had passed since the night on which she'd shown him her willingness to please, and he'd since indicated no desire to lie with her.

Several times, as she'd worked outside, showing Alpia more complicated patterns on the loom, she'd noticed him watching her, looking out from the open doorway of the forge.

He spent day and night there, melting down the spoils their party had gathered from Eanfrith's men.

And hammering!

Evidently, a bandit's iron wasn't good enough for a Norseman to wield. All was being made anew.

Will it be different when I speak his language and we can know one another better?

With all her heart, she hoped so.

Despite their curious circumstances, he'd done much to help her, mending the treadle on her spinning wheel and bringing her several baskets of new-shorn wool. She planned to gather heather and iris leaf, dyeing the fibres dark green. The colour would suit him, as it did her. She might make something for them both, weaving the cloth light and fine for the summer.

She'd shown him her thanks with smiles and tried to touch his arm, but he'd shrunk away at that.

Their food was plentiful, Magnus earning his share of fish and game in return for his work in the forge, but he was yet to take a meal with her and the children. He preferred to eat alone.

Meanwhile, though the other women exchanged whispered stories of their men's virility, she remained untouched in the way that mattered.

His rejection pained her.

It was as if she'd merely dreamt the taste of him on her tongue.

She thought of that now. Thought of him.

If I went to the forge at this very moment, would he bark at me to leave?

There was only one way to find out.

Putting down her knife, she untied her apron and smoothed her skirts. Whatever the outcome, she wouldn't hide from her own husband!

She stepped outside and blinked at the dazzle of bright sunlight, then found herself face to face with the last man she wished to see.

Fecir smirked as Modwen bumped against him and, before she had the chance to dart away, he grasped both her wrists.

"No need to hurry." He grinned, showing his yellow teeth. "I'm paying a visit." Fecir held her firm, grazing his knuckles over her breasts. "You've time to offer a cup of something to your dear old uncle?"

Modwen attempted to wrestle free, but he drove her back through the doorway. Once they were inside, he let her go, appearing triumphant.

Modwen rubbed her wrists and suppressed a scowl, reminding herself to be patient. Fecir had been defending Achnaryrie when he'd received an axe blow to his shoulder. The wound had healed well, and he'd regained modest use of the arm, though he often used it as an excuse to evade harder labour.

"I'll make you some warm chamomile," she conceded, "but then I've things to do." She stoked the fire beneath the pan of water she kept hanging above in the hearth, one eye warily on him. "And my husband to attend to—"

Fecir spat on the floor—on the clean rushes she had spread out only the day before, with dried lavender and rosemary stalks intermixed. "I'm sure you have. Since those devils came, they've every woman sniffing about to please them."

Modwen had a few opinions of her own, thinking the Norsemen over fond of mead and ale, and too boisterousness in their cups, but Fecir's attitude put her in a mind to defend them.

"And have you noticed the work those 'devils' have done for us?" With her pestle, she crushed the chamomile more forcefully than was necessary, reducing the petals almost to dust. "You've eaten what they've provided eagerly enough."

"Decent women turned to whoring themselves for a bit of meat," he sneered. "You couldn't get them in your beds fast enough." His lips curled. "Meat for your bellies and meat for your greedy cunts."

Modwen whirled upon him, smacking him in the chest, pushing him off balance. "You've no honour in you!"

She'd always tried to ignore his taunts, but in this, he'd gone too far. "Magnus is my husband. You've no right to say such things."

Fecir's face darkened.

"I'll speak to you how I like, whore. You were mine to take as wife, though you wriggled out of it to give your favours to these curs." He made a grab for her, pinning her against the table's edge with his body.

She'd been a fool to let him in—to allow herself to be alone with him. The knife was behind her somewhere. If she could reach it, she'd show him that she wouldn't stand for his insults.

"Give me what I want, Modwen, and I'll leave you alone." His voice had a thick rasp to it, inflamed by her struggle.

She turned away, but he leaned in, his breath touching her cheek. Frantically, she skimmed the wooden surface with her fingertips.

"That's it. Hold still while I have a taste of you." He found her breast, squeezing through the cloth of her tunic, then pinching, his fumbling fingers seeking her nipple.

The knife must be at the other end, she realised. His wet lips streaked her throat, moving to the neckline of her tunic. His fingers tugged at the yoke.

"No!" She wanted to shout, but the word came out half-strangled, caught between shock and disbelief. She brought her arms round and tried to push him off, but she was trapped, unable to lever against him.

"No!" She tried again. Better, but not enough.

No one would hear, even though the door was ajar. Repeatedly, she pushed, but his nose pressed into her breast, snuffling at her softness, his tongue probing.

Her third cry was louder, though it seemed to take all her strength to form the sound, leaving her boneless beneath him, choking with horror. He'd pushed his leg hard between hers while his weaker arm groped under layers of linen, ferreting for bare flesh.

As he suckled fiercely, she took an instinctive gasp, drawing air deep into her lungs.

At last, she screamed.

8

There was a roar, as of crashing storm-driven waves, or the rush of wind whirling upon the headland, and the pressing weight lifted from her chest.

In a tangle of arms and legs, Fecir was slumped on the floor, his mouth gaping. A trickle of blood seeped from his nose.

The man towering above Fecir growled as he drew him up, hoisting him to his feet by the front of his tunic. With limbs dangling, Fecir hung suspended, uttering faint whimpers, his eyes wide in his pale face.

Magnus took three strides before hurling Fecir outside.

Seeing the force with which Magnus threw the other man, one thought was clear in her mind. Modwen's stomach twisted.

She staggered forward, clutching at the doorframe. A crowd had gathered, though all kept their distance.

Magnus loomed above Fecir, who hid his face in his arms, cowering, drawing up his legs to protect himself, waiting for the great Norseman's fists to rain their blows.

Magnus's voice was harsh and guttural, as if he were chewing the gristle of Fecir's bones. With a stout kick to Fecir's back, he sent him sprawling in the dirt, then hauled him up again, rolling him over to place his foot on the other's neck.

"Don't! You'll kill him!" Modwen shrieked, her breaths coming in rasps.

Magnus jerked up his head. Her tone was unmistakable, as his own had been—hers aghast with fear, while his spoke of violent intent.

In his face was a fury disproportionate with any she could have imagined, his eyes alight, almost frenzied, filled with hate that surely could not be for Fecir alone.

Magnus was her husband in little more than name, yet he'd heard her distress and come to her aid. Now, he seemed ready to beat Fecir bloody for having touched what was his.

A wracking sob rose within Modwen's chest.

I can't let him do it.

Her knees trembled, but Ailsa was beside her, offering her shoulder, and Eithne, too.

She spoke the words Modwen had only just

begun to learn. Whatever she'd said, it took sudden effect.

Magnus removed his weight from Fecir's neck, though he gave one last kick to the creature at his feet, showing no remorse as Fecir spluttered and groaned.

Eithne spoke again, the clipped, curt Norse that sounded strange, uttered with the delicate melody of their own Pict rhythms. Magnus fixed his stare hard upon Modwen before he turned his back.

When he'd walked away, Eithne drew close, taking Modwen's other arm. She and Ailsa led her back into the hut, making her sit on her bed.

"What did you say?" Modwen asked.

"Only what I needed to." Eithne took up the cup of chamomile and, adding water from the steaming pot, placed it between Modwen's hands.

Eithne shook her head, then sighed deeply. "He vowed to kill him."

Modwen held the cup tightly. "We can't let that happen."

"No, we can't," Eithne agreed. "There are few here who'd shed tears for Fecir"—she looked meaningfully at Modwen—"but we must have order and the same rules for everyone."

Modwen struggled to swallow, her throat growing tight. It was true that Fecir had few allies. He'd been better accepted when Galan was alive—respected, even, when he'd helped in the forge. In recent times, tolerance had waned. He was not loved.

Only her desire to honour Galan had driven Modwen to endure all she had.

Still, she wished Fecir no lasting harm. His life surely hadn't turned out the way he'd hoped it might. That was something with which Modwen could empathise.

"Lie down," said Ailsa. "You've had a shock."

Her gaze wandered to Modwen's tunic, the front of which was torn.

Modwen nodded, her cheeks growing warm. It was shaming for others to know—to see what Galan's uncle was capable of.

"Rest," Eithne agreed. "I'll find Alpia and Taran and keep them busy for some hours."

It was a relief to close her eyes, while Ailsa sat beside her, smoothing her hair.

So much seemed to lay heavy on her, and she didn't know where to begin. She'd thought marrying the Norseman would bring an end to her troubles—or some of them, at least.

One thing must be true, she thought. *He must care about me.*

He'd come when she'd needed him.

No one else.

But he had come.

9

Reaching the forest's edge, Magnus laid his forehead to the cool bark of an oak.

Breathe. Just breathe.

He concentrated on drawing air into his lungs, then exhaling slowly. His pulse was still racing in his ears, his chest heaving.

A terrible fury had seized him like a man possessed. He'd almost killed that maggot, Fecir.

He'd wanted to stamp his foot hard into the scum's face, crushing his skull. His head pounded at the thought of it.

Modwen's scream had been like that in his nightmares—those gut-wrenching dreams of Solveig, struggling and screaming, from which he woke soaked in sweat. No matter how fast he ran, he could never reach her in time.

The sight that had met him entering Modwen's hut, had stirred him into a burning rage—a crimson haze of anger that only violence would satisfy.

Not that the bastard didn't deserve to die, but Magnus knew better than to serve up justice on the point of his temper. If he had issue with another man's conduct towards his wife, he should have issued a challenge to the *holmgang*. It was senseless, of course, since the worm was no match for him. There would have been no honour in such a duel, though it was their tradition—their method of justice.

Justice.

The word had a hollow ring.

There had been none for Solveig.

The *úlfhéðinn* had left her broken like a child's doll—swollen-faced, twisted on the saturated earth, the birds picking at her flesh.

Wolf-skins, they called them, for the cloaks they wore, or berserks, for they lost all humanity in their trance-like rage. Animals, not men, they howled and bit the edge of their shields. With no fear of fire nor iron, it was said a berserk could blunt his opponent's weapon by looking at it.

Magnus swallowed bile, bitter in his mouth.

Such men deserved no accolade, for what bravery was there in attacking a woman alone in the woods, or the elderly they'd slain that day, before running for the wooded mountainside above Skalanes.

He'd begged Brandr to gather men and pursue

them, to scour every possible hiding place until they'd bloodied their weapons. His old friend had shared his ire, but for all their skill and strength, the men of Skalanes lacked familiarity with the mountains. To enter those wild lands would be to encounter certain ambush.

Magnus knew the wisdom of it, but the fact did naught to assuage his outrage and despair, fuelled by knowledge of his inaction.

He'd not been there to protect her and could do nothing to bring her back. The poisoned barb lay buried deep and had festered. He found no comfort —not in his sons, nor in the comradeship of those he'd known all his life. Even sleep brought no respite, and the agony bit him anew on awakening.

Only in the forge did he find some solace, beating his sorrow and unspoken fury into the metal. Training with the weapons he created, he fought recklessly, until no other would parry with him for fear of tasting the sharp edge of his blade.

Brandr had drawn him aside, reminding him that his sons needed their father, for didn't they also grieve? He knew it to be true, but looking at them only made him think of Solveig, and the pain was too great. Solveig's mother had taken care of them in those early years.

He'd failed his wife. She'd done nothing to deserve the horror of her death, so the blame must be his. In some way, he'd displeased the gods and been made to pay for his wrongdoing.

Turning about, he rested his back against the trunk of the ancient tree. Somewhere above, a song thrush was offering up its melody. Towards the cliffs, the sky was a haze of blue. He'd been so intent on shutting himself away, he'd hardly bothered to survey the landscape of Achnaryrie.

The forest smelt fragrant. Dropping to his haunches, he brushed his hand over the blooms of a delicate flower. Swathes of violet stretched out from beneath the oak, across the woodland.

Skalanes's woodlands had something similar, he was sure. Solveig had picked them at about this time of year.

Had these tiny bells been here on the day their men had brought back Brandr wounded? It had been too dark to see much, but their scent was strong.

Flowers! When did I ever notice flowers?

Magnus passed his hand over his face. Nothing seemed to make sense. It hadn't for a long time.

Absentmindedly, he touched the hem of his tunic. It was the one he'd been wearing on the first day they'd arrived in Achnaryrie, and it had been torn. Now, neat stitches brought the ragged edges together.

He'd paid no regard when he'd donned it that morning, had given no thought to the hands that had laid it out for him. In the forge, he usually just wore his leggings and a leather apron if he was working with molten metal—but he'd wanted to see Brandr. The injury was healing well, while Bjorn's fever had at last abated.

Magnus fingered the material again.

The other women would be with her, wouldn't they?

Even so, he should go back. For some purpose, the gods had once more made him a husband.

Perhaps something did matter.

10

In her sleep, her eyelids flickered, and she sighed. Smoothing back her hair, he touched her cheek, and she murmured. His name? It had sounded something like it.

He wondered how to rouse her, or if he should, but the choice was taken from him as she turned her head into his calloused palm. Before he had the chance to withdraw, she opened her eyes.

Finding him so close, she shrank back, her expression guarded, remembering—he supposed—the aggression he'd shown little more than an hour ago.

A portion of the previous day's broth remained. After some hesitation, she took the bowl he offered but continued to eye him warily.

"Come," he said when she'd eaten the last mouthful.

He'd filled the wooden tub and set the soap out.

She looked across the room, then back to him, but didn't move.

"Come," he said again, drawing the fur from her shoulders. With the fire stoked high, the room was warm enough.

With his help, she sat up, and, taking her hand, he led her to the centre of the room.

He unclasped the belt from her waist, then bent to the hem of her long, outer dress. Obediently, she raised her arms so that the gown slipped easily over her head as he lifted it. By the flicker of the fire, her outline was visible beneath her thin-woven shift—the indentation of her waist, the flare of her hip and shapely leg.

Magnus had intended nothing but to offer food and a bath, that she might know her comfort mattered.

Yet, his desire stirred.

Crossing her arms to either side, Modwen raised the remaining garment. As her nakedness was revealed, she loosened her dark hair from its braid, and it unravelled in soft curls, tumbling over her shoulders.

He'd been too long starved of such a sight. Standing before him, she did nothing to conceal herself, and he drank in her sensual beauty.

When their eyes met, what passed between them he could not have described—something of pride, uncertainty, and its opposite.

Modwen steadied herself upon his arm and

stepped into the water. She eased under, lowering her shoulders, then her head beneath its warmth. Rising, she slicked back the dripping hair from her face.

He drew up a stool to sit close and offered her the soap. She merely shook her head and closed her eyes.

The room was quiet but for the crackle of flames.

He watched the subtle rise and fall of her breaths, the water rippling where it met her ribs. She appeared to be made of some fine ceramic, so pale were her limbs, and so unblemished.

Tendrils of her hair hung damply, curling upon her cheek, over her neck and collarbone. The fire-light danced upon the slick sheen of her skin, casting a rosy glow over the lush curve of her breasts.

A sudden flaming awareness clenched his stomach.

She belonged to him.

He was her husband and her master.

He hadn't wanted this, hadn't wanted her, but impulse brought his palm to the fullness of her flesh. She drew sudden breath and half-opened her lids, looking at him through her lashes. Without moving, he held her, cupping the weight of her breast, beneath which her heartbeat fluttered.

So smooth.

He drew his thumb over one large, rosebud

nipple—softly, back and forth. She leaned into his hand's embrace, and her lips parted.

Again, their eyes met. Hers had grown wider, darker. She seemed to beckon him with her eyes, but she was also trembling, waiting for him to show her what would happen next. Her breaths were shallow and rapid, as from a bird held in his fist, over which he held all power.

I want her.

Desire struck him forcefully. He knew only that he must kiss her.

With her head captured suddenly between his hands, she whimpered. She made as if to push him away, but he brought his lips to hers, and she yielded to his possession, opening to the sudden, crushing need of his mouth and the exploration of his tongue.

He cradled her head, drawing her closer. He dropped his other hand low, fitting it into the slender curve of her back. She held her arms between them, as if part of her would still resist, though the rest of her body was languid.

Deepening his kiss, he stroked her tongue, then pulled back, teasing with his teeth before crushing her to him again. Having begun, he could not cease. She was melting for him, moaning under his lips, so very willing.

In one sweep, he lifted her, his arm beneath her knees, the cascading water wetting his tunic and trousers. She was dazed as he carried her, as if entranced, submitting to his wishes.

He laid her upon her pallet, and her bruised lips parted once more, inviting his kiss.

Her body was everything he wanted—pale against the dark sheepskins, rounded and firm, her legs slender, and her sex waiting for him.

He would not deny himself.

Quickly, he shed his clothes and pressed his nakedness to her—chill beneath his warmth. Her arms curled about his neck, pulling him into her own hungry kiss—pulling his heat into herself, so that her breasts brushed the hair of his chest.

He had no desire to wait, but nor did he wish to hurt her. Having stroked through the soft curls of her mound, he entered her with his finger.

While her skin was cool, she was hot inside, and she quivered, arching and lifting.

She mewed weakly when he withdrew, and held still as he moved over her. He desired to give her the full thrust of his cock but made himself go slowly, nudging forward. She stretched around him, her hands clasped around his back.

By the gods! So tight!

He feared he'd spill immediately.

Hot and wet, and soft!

He gritted his teeth, having not yet given her even half his length, but she shifted beneath, angling so that he slid deeper.

By Thor and Odin, I am undone!

He growled, pushing the final distance, and Modwen gasped as his hilt finally came to rest against her fur.

Panting, he held still, feeling the rise and fall of her breasts and the slickness of her cream trickling over his bollocks. If he moved again, it would be over.

A man's prowess resided in many things, not least of which was his potency with a woman and a worthy ride upon his manhood, but there was naught Magnus could think of to steer him to a longer journey.

Breathing softly, Modwen lowered her hand, tracing the curve of his buttock, coming to rest where the muscle met his thigh. Her fingertips brushed lightly, and her eyes were twin points of light, fixed upon his own.

"Don't!" he groaned, and then, "I must!"

Quickly, he withdrew and thrust, his outpouring already upon him. He managed but one more plunging into her sheath before he tensed, burying his face in her neck.

She uttered a cry as he surged, finishing deep, placing his full weight upon her.

Too late, he realised he'd failed to curb himself —taking his pleasure abruptly, without due consideration for hers. More than that, his penetration of her body had brought a strange stirring of emotion.

How she gazed at me!

Rolling away, he gave a deep sigh. The pleasure

had been intense—more than he'd known for so long—but a disturbing prickle began behind his eyes, and the old, tight feeling in his chest returned. He remembered why he'd wanted to avoid this. There were too many memories.

Sitting up, he reached for his clothes.

Don't look at her.

He stood, keeping his back to Modwen. If he turned, who knew what flood of feelings would overwhelm him—desperate, dark, terrible feelings. A parching dryness rose in his throat, a searing, choking edge.

Not now. Keep it locked away.

"Magnus?" She spoke his name softly. One word, filled with yearning.

He knew what she wanted from him, but he couldn't give her that. Better for her to realise now and temper her expectations. Kinder to leave and pretend this hadn't happened. Closing the door, he ignored her muffled sob.

11

Turning her face into the pelts, Modwen spent her tears in ragged sobs, the ache of loneliness washing over her.

At last, with swollen eyes, she stayed her heaving breaths. The children would soon return. Eithne had taken them, how many hours ago? They mustn't see her like this.

And what was 'this', other than self-pity?

She rose, donning her clothes, and went to splash her face. The water in the tub was still warm. It would do for Alpia and Taran.

A stab of pain threatened her again, but she pushed it aside.

What had gone wrong?

She'd understood the way he'd looked at her when she'd stood in her shift, his gaze devouring her through the flimsy material. She'd known he desired her, and been glad, yearning for the connection that would bond them as man and wife.

Deeper regard—love—would come later; not just for him but for them both. But the first step of the journey would be taken through the tempest of passion. They would cling together, and he'd feel the shelter of her arms.

At first, baring herself to him, she'd worried that he'd hurt her. He was sizeable in all things—not just his hammer arm—and she'd given no other man her favour since Galan's death.

In fact, Magnus's touch had quickly aroused her, ensuring the slickness needed to ease their union. Her gasps had been not of fright nor pain, but of pleasure, and she'd readily raised her hips to take him deeper. What she might have offered through duty alone, she gave gladly.

She surmised that it had been long since he'd enjoyed a woman, for the coupling was no sooner begun than ended. How many thrusts had he managed? Three, mayhap four?

A disappointment, yes, but such things happened.

It was his manner afterwards that had torn her asunder—as if he were ashamed and regretful. Barely had he taken his release before he'd risen from her side. Not a single endearment had he whispered. No matter whether she understood, the tone of his voice would have told her what she needed to know.

There had been no tender caress. He'd simply rolled away, without a word, without looking back.

This much she meant to him—a body to be taken at his convenience, then disregarded.

If this Norseman had a heart, it beat behind cold walls of stone.

12

Modwen bid the children sit and ladled out their porridge. *Dagmal,* Magnus called it. He'd already collected his portion, taking it to eat in the forge. He didn't seem inclined to share her table, nor anything more intimate.

Bearing his rejection was humiliating but, in other ways, she couldn't fault him. Their trenchers were always full, since Magnus's skills were bartered for meat and fish. Taran and Alpia still scavenged the shoreline for limpets and crab, and the seaweed that was good in stew, but more from habit than necessity.

Thanks to the Norsemen, Achnaryrie's grain stores had been replenished—with rye and barley purchased from other settlements along the coastline in exchange for luxuries on their boats. There was even talk of buying beehives, for honeycomb and to make candles—though Modwen could see nothing wrong with using fish oil for their lamps, as they'd always done.

With their herds of livestock now thriving, Olav was directing the men to build a byre for the cows alongside pens for sheep and goats. She'd given her share of labour, as they all had, collecting larger stones and pebbles from the beach, filling buckets for hauling up the cliffs on rope.

Taran spent most of his time in the forge. Training, he'd said proudly. No meal gathering went by without him sharing what he'd learned.

Whatever the Norseman's feelings for her, he seemed to harbour no ill-will towards her children.

"Magnus says he's going to help me make my own short-handled sword and show me how to wield it," Taran said, speaking between mouthfuls of creamy oats. "A scabbard, too."

Alpia pouted. "I could do that, couldn't I, Mother? I'm almost as big as Taran." She sucked thoughtfully on her spoon. "Although, mayhap I could make something small, that doesn't need so much of the hammer." Her face lit. "A brooch!"

Modwen smoothed her daughter's hair. It was hardly for her to say, but Magnus had been patient with Alpia, letting her watch as he worked. "When he's less busy, you might ask," she allowed.

Taran eyed his sister. "I don't suppose you even know what's inside a scabbard."

"I do! It's made from leather."

"Only on the outside." Taran scraped the last of

the oats from his bowl. "You put fleece next to the blade, to keep it from rusting, wrapped round in wood. See how much I know, and you don't!"

Alpia bit her lip and said nothing, but looked as if she might cry.

"Of course, I'm learning the Norse, as well," Taran said. "I've got to know the words, Magnus says."

"We're all learning, aren't we," Modwen chided.

"Yes." Alpia brightened. "Alarik says I pronounce the words just like a *Norske* girl."

Taran shrugged and stood. "Magnus and I are going into the forest today, to find wood for axe handles." He looked expectantly at Modwen. "We need grease to put on them afterwards—*flot,* it's called." He gave Alpia a sidelong glance, to make sure she'd heard him using the Norse. "You can get some, can't you, Mother? Magnus says goose fat is best, or from a pig."

"I'll see what I can do." Modwen smiled indulgently. It made her happy to see Taran so excited. Whatever fear she'd had that he'd resent this Norseman, it had proven unfounded. She only wished Alpia might not feel left out.

"Take your sister with you." She gave Taran her most serious expression. "There's no reason why she can't help find the right wood and help you in carrying it."

Taran grimaced, but Alpia leapt up with a grin.

"Just make sure you're no trouble, and do everything Magnus tells you."

She managed to give them both a squeeze around the shoulders before they sped off, still bickering.

Modwen set the bowls aside. Despite their squabbles, the children were content. She wished she could say the same for herself.

Near a sennight had passed since Magnus had bedded her. Now, he was civil but kept her at arm's length.

Each night, upon her pallet, she touched where he had touched, imagining his hands upon her body—his manhood stretching her, sliding into her warmth.

How could he not want this as she did?

Something had brought him to her before, and she wished she could recapture it.

At least Fecir had not bothered her again. Eithne had told the jarl of his assault, and Brandr had bade him stay away. What punishment there would be if he did not, she couldn't say, but Fecir had kept his distance. She was satisfied to leave it at that.

Now, goose fat!

Modwen wracked her memory. Myrna would have some. Hadn't she given a salve of birch bark oil mixed with goose fat this past winter, when the children had taken unwell? Modwen had smeared it on their chests, and it had done much to relieve the coughing.

She knew where Myrna might be. As their most experienced healer, she changed the jarl's wound dressing every morning, and that of his brother.

Modwen looked about her for the narrow strips of cloth she'd woven with Alpia, showing her trickier formations on the little handloom before letting her try on the large frame. They'd make attractive bands to wear around the head, or to sew onto the yoke of a tunic. She'd take some for Myrna.

Outside, the weather was fine again. Another good day for the men to fish and hunt, or to continue their planting of the meadows.

As Modwen passed the forge, she couldn't resist peeking in. Magnus had left one of the double doors open wide. There was no need to lock anything away, since no thievery would go undetected. Besides which, these Norsemen seemed to have a strict code of honour. Whatever she thought of their marauding ways, she couldn't deny the strength of their brotherhood. Even Magnus, who chose his own company above that of others, was greeted heartily by his fellow Vikings.

Modwen had avoided the forge, yet it was the place where her husband slept and ate and spent all his time.

A compulsion came over her to enter.

Just for a few moments, and I shan't touch anything.

Inside, it was warm, the furnace embers still glowing.

It was evident he'd been busy. Smooth arrowheads lay piled on the earthen shelves, and a selection of farming tools besides. Some were in designs she'd not seen before—forks with thick prongs and shovelling blades of deep curvature. It gave her some pride, knowing they were his handiwork.

In the far corner was a straw-stuffed mattress, topped with the blanket he'd asked of her. There was also a pillow, which was not of her giving. Kneeling, she set aside her resolution and brought it to her nose.

It was feather-filled and smelt of him—leather and perspiration.

She placed her cheek where his had been and wondered who'd given it to him. She might have done so herself but had been reluctant to make his sleeping arrangements more comfortable than the alternative—her own bed.

Has he found another woman already, and she's given him this?

Heat flashed through her at the thought. She'd share her husband with nobody! She tossed the pillow down, almost hoping it might burst a little and let some feathers flutter out.

When it didn't, she made everything neat again and gave a deep sigh.

Whatever trouble kept him from her bed, she didn't think it came in female form.

Still, a twinge of jealousy remained, for someone had given him what it was her duty to provide.

Enough.

She rose to her feet.

I shouldn't be here.

The door banged, and it grew suddenly darker. The wind must have swung it shut. Light filtered in from a hole in the turfed roof, through which the furnace smoke rose, and the embers cast their own glow, but the farther reaches of the room were shadowy. The forge had no windows.

Moving forward, Modwen hit her toe on the large, upturned log upon which the anvil sat.

Damnation!

She rubbed her foot and resolved to stand still a few moments to let her eyes adjust. Patience was a virtue, as Father Godfrey liked to remind them.

It didn't take long. Soon, she was able to make out Magnus's tools, laid out nearby. Tracing the edge of the workbench, she groped towards the centre of the room but paused halfway.

What was that?

She strained to listen.

A mouse?

There had been a shuffling sound.

She squinted, trying to see through the various shades of grey. It was quiet again, but something had moved, she was certain.

A hard pounding began in her chest, making it

difficult to breathe. Through the thickness of the dark, there was a sour smell—of unwashed sweat and old herring.

"Who's there?" Her voice was eaten, and no answer came.

From above, there was a sudden scuttering and flapping—a bird or a bat, caught under the timbers. With a start, Modwen rushed forward, no longer caring whether she bumped into anything, just wanting to get outside.

She cursed again as her hip banged an unseen corner, then yelped, running into another obstacle. Its face was pale, and its teeth yellow. Two arms came tight around her.

13

Before Modwen could scream, he clamped his fingers over her mouth. She struggled, and he pressed harder, pushing her head so violently that she feared her neck would snap.

She wanted to yell, but her throat was drawn back so tightly she could barely breathe.

As dim as the room had been, it was growing dimmer.

"No Norse bastard to save you now." The voice was sneering. "No one here at all." He bent her back farther. "You won't be so high and mighty when I've finished with you."

Again, she tried to twist away, but the side of his hand crushed her nose.

If he doesn't stop, I won't be able to...

She went limp.

Flailing one arm, she prayed that she'd alight on

something—anything! All those tools, but she couldn't reach them.

Instead, she pushed at him, but he was unyielding. Whatever strength he had was concentrated in this moment.

I'm going to...

Something inside her slipped.

She was having trouble thinking, and there was a horrible taste in her mouth. One of his fingers had worked between her lips. Herring, most definitely, and something else—pungent.

Her teeth grazed his skin.

Bite him!

She didn't know if she could remember how, or make it happen.

It's a carrot, she thought, and then wanted to laugh.

As she brought her jaws down hard, he shrieked.

A hard, stinging blow hit her across the cheek, sending her to her knees. Gasping for air, she didn't understand why she was on the floor.

And then he kicked her—hard, in the ribs.

"Vicious bitch!" He aimed his foot again and caught her on the shoulder.

Crawl away, where he won't find me.

Was it darker down here than it had been when she'd been standing? He must have been able to see her, for he landed another boot, this time to her thigh, and she yelped.

I won't let him.

I won't!

She kept crawling, but he was behind her.

"I'll kick out your teeth." His voice was a snarl.

She was going to be sick, or stop breathing. Terror and nausea fought inside her.

And then she found the edge of something with her hands. She was back almost where she'd begun, next to the anvil.

Her eyes prickled.

I can't find my way out.

He was shuffling closer, feeling ahead with his foot.

Perhaps he couldn't see her after all.

His toes nudged her knee, and she acted on impulse rather than thought. Flinging herself forward, she encircled his shins, and yanked hard, sideways.

Pull him off his feet...and then what?

She wasn't sure, only knowing that she must.

He grunted as he fell, toppling over Modwen's back. His legs rose. There was a thud and a strange groan, then the thump of his body to the floor.

She scrabbled away, heaving great breaths. Never had her heart pounded like this, so violent. Her head spun, and she trembled all over.

I must get out.

She crawled a little more, but all her strength was gone. Her forehead was resting on the floor, and then there were no more thoughts.

She was truly in the dark.

14

Emerging from the forest, the children pointed in the direction of the beach, chattering excitedly. Low tide always brought crabs to the rockpools. To make themselves understood, they wriggled their arms and ran from side to side.

He nodded his permission and waved them away, smiling as they bounded towards the cliff path.

The time had passed pleasantly, both children being keen to please him, darting from tree to tree, looking for an oak suitable to cut from—straight-grained and hard, it was the best choice of wood for a sturdy axe handle.

On the way back, seeing Taran making faces at his sister, Magnus had swept him up, sitting him on the lower branch of a birch and, with his feet dangling, Alpia had jumped up to tickle them.

Magnus had laughed, and the rising chuckle in

his chest had surprised him, as if he'd forgotten how to make such a sound.

In the past week, he'd noticed small things changing—not just in Achnaryrie, but in himself. When he woke, it was to the familiar jolt of remembrance and pain, but to another feeling also—that there was work to be done, and that he was needed to do it.

Something else, as well, if he were honest.

Something he could no longer deny.

It lightened his spirit, knowing she was close by. Yesterday, he'd touched her fingers as she'd passed him the bowl of *grøt*. She'd looked up at him, briefly, before glancing away.

Her eyes!

Though they were dark, where Solveig's had been blue, there was an intensity to Modwen's, and his heart trembled.

The world had been a bleak and bitter place, a perpetual winter in which his blood had turned to ice.

The Norns had drawn a hard fate for him, from the Well of Urðr, but it seemed another destiny had now been cast.

He'd been afraid to open his frozen heart, but only a fool would ignore this second chance. Knowing it, he'd be twice the fool to waste any more time.

He was resolved to find Modwen and, by Thor's thunder, he'd show her that he'd come to his senses.

With Odin's blessing, she would see that his intentions were true—that he would no more fail her.

With the two long branches under his arms, he headed back.

Magnus pushed the door with his foot.

Strange that it's closed.

Hadn't he left it open purposefully, to bring in warmth from the morning sun, and fresh air?

There had been a musty smell, now overlaid with something else—fish? He frowned, unable to put his finger on it.

He drew both doors wide so that sunlight filled the darkened space, and deposited the wood. Dust motes whirled, disturbed by the sudden motion.

Nothing seemed amiss, but there was a palpable sense of someone having been here. Mayhap Garth. He'd said he'd call by, wanting his dagger sharpening. No one wielded a whetstone like Magnus.

Garth would have to bide, though, for hadn't Magnus other matters to attend? A comely wife waited, and the children would be long busy on the shore.

Then, there was a whimper—a pitiful mewling sound, from the far side of the room, near his bed.

She was curled, her head buried upon her knees. In three strides he reached her, raising her from the floor, gathering Modwen secure to his chest.

She was shivering. Like a child woken from a bad dream, her face was ashen, her lips bloodless. As if she were still in that place between waking and sleep, she was unable to distinguish what was about her.

Had she fallen? A bruise was blooming beneath her eye.

"I'm here." He wrapped her tightly, and she clung to him, resting her forehead against his torso.

He didn't move, smoothing her hair, waiting for the tremors in her body to subside, giving her his warmth and strength.

"Are you hurt?"

Her eyes welled with tears. She shook her head and tried to speak, but her voice broke. Her gaze was fixed across the room, to where a figure slumped beneath the anvil.

He saw it now—the neck at an unnatural angle, and a dark stain soaking the earthen floor.

Cold dread snaked his spine.

Was it?

Magnus needed to be sure.

Drawing Modwen from his arms, he bent to examine the body.

Fecir's mouth gaped in silence, and crimson oozed from the back of his skull. Magnus touched his fingers to the matted hair, and the head lolled to one side, the eyes staring dull. A trickle of blood ran from his ear.

Modwen gave a great gulping sob and stumbled away, looking from Magnus to the thing that had once been a man. She held her hand to her mouth, staggering to the door, and there, she retched.

The first time Magnus had killed a man, hadn't he done the same? The memory was dim, but he was sure it had been so. Euphoria had carried him at first—exhilaration at felling his enemies without sustaining a scratch upon his own skin.

Only later had he been overtaken by nausea.

He placed his hand lightly upon Modwen's back, offering his presence as she spat the last of her *dagmal* onto the ground.

He hardly needed to ask for explanation. It was easy to surmise, and if he'd dealt with Fecir properly the first time, this would never have happened.

The blame was his.

A man with *drengr* showed not only bravery on the battlefield but had the strength to do what was right.

Modwen was capable, but she needed him. The tightness in his chest was anger—that he'd failed, again, to protect the woman in his care.

Magnus couldn't bring himself to feel sorry for Fecir's death, but there would be consequences.

Whatever punishment was due, he would take upon himself.

Already, two of the women were approaching, warily, drawn by the sight of Modwen's distress.

There could be no hiding.

Eithne passed a scrap of cloth from her pocket, which Modwen took gratefully, wiping her mouth.

"You're unwell," Ailsa said. "You should sit."

Modwen nodded, then shook her head, and wished she hadn't. Her left eye ached, and her cheekbone was tender.

The women were staring at her aghast, casting accusing looks at Magnus.

"'Twas an accident." How light-headed she felt. As if the ground was rising to meet her. Her legs wobbled, and Magnus's arms came swiftly to her waist.

"Here," Eithne directed, pointing to the stool before the door of Modwen's dwelling. "You need water."

Ailsa darted into the house, returning with a cup from which Modwen sipped.

"Do you need our help?" Eithne crouched, turning her body so that Magnus might not see her speak.

Modwen sniffed and gave a strange half-laugh, then winced. It seemed her lip had split.

"Our husbands are strict, but to beat you like this!" Eithne's eyes flashed with disapproval.

Modwen pressed her palm to her forehead. Everything felt so jumbled, but she remembered unbalancing Fecir, and then a terrible crack and thud as he'd fallen.

After that, had she fainted? When she'd come to, it'd been easier to see, the sun having risen high enough that its beams came through the smoke hole in the roof.

That was when she'd seen him—unmoving, twisted in that horrible way, his eyes fixed upwards but no longer seeing.

Dead.

Murdered.

And the penalty would be her own death.

15

Eithne faced Magnus boldly.

"What happened?" she demanded, speaking in his own tongue. "Isn't Modwen a willing wife, wishing to please you?"

Magnus knew what he must say, and he hoped the gods would forgive his falsehoods.

"Fetch our jarl, for he must see justice done. An unworthy cur lies dead, and it was his foul advances upon my wife that brought his end. I found him attacking in violent lust and sent him sprawling. I needed no weapon to spill his brains, for Thor guided the wretch to fall heavy on my anvil."

"Dead?" Eithne's eyes widened, and she spoke quickly to the other, sending her to fetch Brandr, urging her to run. "Who is dead?"

Magnus's lip curled. "Fecir was his name. The uncle of my wife's late husband—more worm than man, and fitting that the worms shall now feast on him."

Eithne paled. She looked from Magnus to Modwen, and her brow furrowed in remembrance.

"You threw Fecir from the house, shouting that you'd kill him." She cringed.

"Magnus?" Modwen attempted to stand, but her legs buckled.

"Put her to bed," Eithne said. "Carry her, quickly. She's in no condition to remain out here. I'll ask Myrna to attend to her injuries."

Modwen was as limp as a doll in his arms as he laid her on the pallet. Despite the sun's warmth, her skin was cool. He pushed back the hair from her face and offered her more water, but she seemed unable to swallow. He pulled a sheepskin to cover her.

More than ever, his mind was set.

He'd failed Solveig all those years ago, not having been there to defend her. And he'd almost failed again. Who knew what Modwen had endured? Would Fecir have killed her? The cur had little to live for, and revenge was a tempting dish.

Magnus cursed himself.

A fine husband he was! Never where he needed to be!

But he'd do his duty now.

The Pict laws were strange, he'd heard, and their punishments severe. He wouldn't allow

Modwen to suffer further. Any penalty would be his.

Returning outside, Magnus found Brandr waiting for him. A small crowd had gathered, whispering and pointing. Brandr's expression was grim, while Eithne stood apart, talking in hushed tones with the other women.

"You've seen?" Magnus nodded towards the forge.

"Aye." Brandr narrowed his eyes. He lowered his voice and drew Magnus a little farther off. "You killed him?"

"The weasel was lusting after my wife again. What should I have done? Poured him ale to quench his thirst after the deed was done?"

"And she didn't encourage him?"

"Nay!" Magnus hissed. "She had no liking for his attentions."

"But it wasn't the first time they'd met alone." Brandr paused. He seemed to consider his next words carefully.

"Eithne tells me there was a prior agreement, of sorts, before we arrived. A man may tear his teeth when his claim upon a woman is forsaken."

"If there was any arrangement, Modwen wanted none of it, I'm sure." Magnus thrust out his chest. "Fecir was a boneless snake. Little wonder the cur couldn't take a single push. That he stumbled and hit his head was the will of the gods. On the anvil, too! If Thor didn't have a hand in that, then who did?"

"You may be right, but such an answer won't serve." Brandr sighed. "The man was ill-loved, as I understand, and Modwen and her children were his only relations, so there's no family to be reconciled with payment of weregild. But we aren't in Skalanes, and I must be seen to observe the laws of this place."

"As you say." Magnus lowered his head. "And I shall submit to your judgement."

"Here, an eye must be paid with an eye, but you're too important to forfeit, Magnus. If you'd called a challenge to *holmgang,* in answer to your wife's assault, no man would have questioned it, but for him to die in this manner, in your own forge—" Brandr raised his chin. "No matter my own feeling, and that of your warrior brothers, I must give punishment, for what future can we build without trust between us and those of Achnaryrie? We're superior in strength, so we must guard our tempers."

Magnus grunted his assent.

"You will dig the burial place, then offer your back for twenty lashes." Brandr glanced at those standing not far off, whose eyes were upon them, awaiting their jarl's command, wishing to hear what justice would be served.

"Had I not this injury," Brandr touched lightly beneath his ribs, "I would deliver the strokes myself. Instead, Olav shall be my arm, and I shall tell him not to spare you."

With a single nod, Magnus acknowledged Brandr's words.

Modwen woke with a heavy head, as if some great weight had come to press on her, and there was no pushing it away. Bringing her hand to her cheek, she sucked in a breath. One eye didn't wish to open, and her lip felt swollen. She licked it tentatively, testing the size of the cut with the tip of her tongue and tasting the congealment of blood.

Her ribs and leg hurt, too, but she couldn't remember why.

One of the women had visited her, hadn't they? Myrna—placing salve on her bruises.

She eased herself upright, lowering her feet to the floor.

To the side was the tunic she'd been sewing for Magnus. Wincing, she walked over, picking it up to rub the cloth between her fingers.

Where were the children? It must be late in the day, for there was hardly any light.

She remembered. Magnus had taken Alpia and Taran into the forest, and she'd intended to see Myrna—goose fat, wasn't it? On a whim, she'd gone into the forge, wanting to see where Magnus was working, wanting to feel closer to him.

It had been so dark.

Oh God!

She gripped the table's edge. In a sudden, terrible rush, the memory washed over her—a rough palm over her mouth and her neck forced back. She hadn't been able to breathe nor push him away. And then, she'd bitten what was in her mouth.

Was that when she'd fallen?

She'd been on the floor, and someone had kicked her.

Another image came rushing in—of a dead face.

Fecir!

Modwen fought down a returning wave of nausea.

He'd hit his head, hadn't he?

Because of her.

He was dead, by her hand!

Modwen slumped against the wall.

What happened to those who broke God's word? It was a commandment, wasn't it? Thou shalt not kill.

Father Godfrey had described Hell—demons and everlasting torture, fire and pain.

Mercy upon her!

What should she do?

Admit her guilt?

But to who? Father Godfrey or to their new jarl? Brandr didn't believe in their god, so would it count?

She shivered, glancing to the far corners, where the gloom clung thickest.

There were other things to fear besides the monk's teachings. Beneath what she knew of Christian faith there lingered memories of older belief—of dark forces rising from the shadows to claim those black of heart.

Modwen grasped her throat and screwed tight her eyes.

She didn't dare look.

Serpents or devils, something fearsome would drag her to the punishment she deserved.

God was merciful, so maybe her people would be, too. Atonement was her only hope.

Perhaps, then, she would be spared.

16

Stripped to the waist, Magnus stood within the livestock pen.

Dusk was upon the headland, turning the lower reaches of the sky violet shades, threaded through with amber. The sea glittered beneath like molten steel, hot from Magnus's own furnace.

They'd erected a makeshift timber pole, about which his wrists were tied.

There was a crowd, though Eithne had insisted the children be kept inside.

Steinn stood close, his usual merriment replaced by an expression of disbelief. Ragnar and Thorolf looked on with eyes of winter ice. They would not approve of this punishment, for was a man not entitled to defend his wife?

Yet, Magnus understood; Brandr could not let the matter pass.

Achnaryrie was under Norse rule, but they

needed the respect and trust of its people. Brandr could not simply set aside the laws of this land.

He stood before them, speaking clear and calm. "A man has died this day, and the one before you admits his hand struck the fatal wound. However, knowing Magnus to be a man of honesty, I consider the deed not murder, but mischance—"

A murmur rippled through those gathered. Some shook their heads, while others nodded, stony-faced.

"And wrought under circumstances with which every man can sympathise," Brandr finished.

Someone said: "The cur was asking for trouble. I'd have done the same."

Another, to his left, declared: "Killed outright, and in the forge. The Norseman's guilty!"

Brandr raised himself to full height, that they might know who was in charge. "Norse law dictates payment to the grieving family for their loss, and no other punishment, but I've vowed to uphold justice according to Achnaryrie's customs. I see no wilful intent to take another's life—only a man protecting his wife's honour, and who forgot the strength of his arm. Thus, I decree no penalty of death. Twenty lashes will be his price for wrongdoing, as your law allows."

Amidst muttering, Olav stepped forward, brandishing a length of ship's rope. Unbraided at the ends, it had been tied into several knots.

"May every man and woman witness my

authority"—Brandr scanned the surrounding faces—"and Magnus Thorensson's acceptance of my judgement."

Hush fell upon them as Olav took his stance, dropping his arm low, the tails of the rope trailing to the dirt.

Magnus fixed his gaze on the horizon.

Odin is watching. He sees and approves.

There is nothing to fear—only pain to be endured.

He regretted nothing.

A sudden gust fluttered through the far-off forest, shivering birch and oak, and the wind brought a gull's cry.

Then, there was a swish of air.

Magnus stiffened. Where each knot struck, his flesh protested.

There was a pause as Olav adjusted his position, and Magnus braced for the second lash. It came harder than the first, taking the breath from his body.

The third fell quickly, and he jerked with clenched teeth, the hollow inside him fist-tight. He stiffened, waiting for the next. When it came, he grunted, straining against his bonds. The sixth saw him groan in earnest, for flames darted hot beneath the skin.

Among the crowd, there was a gasp and a stifled whimper. Several of the watchers had turned away.

By the ninth, it took all his discipline to keep from crying out.

He was no stranger to pain. Hadn't he enough scars and burns upon his flesh in proof of that? Yet, he slumped.

And then, he no longer counted the strokes.

From some distant place, a woman screamed.

His wrists were still tied, but the beat of the rope upon his back had ceased.

With tears streaming, a sobbing woman held his head.

Modwen?

Her face swam before him, and the world went dark.

He roused to a feeling of stiffness through his body and something wet and heavy on his back. His bladder was demanding relief, but as he shifted, he gasped with pain.

Groaning, he extended his hand. Was there a pot? It was too dark to see.

Instead, he grasped a fistful of soft hair and a warm, womanly shoulder. Someone was lying next to him. She helped him sit up, then placed a receptacle where he needed it. When he was done, she eased him back onto his front. Fleetingly, he thought of a question he needed to ask, but then it was gone. She stroked his hair, and his eyes closed again.

The next time he woke, it was daylight.

"Drink this." A cup of hot liquid was pressed to his lips—a bitter brew.

Magnus turned his head into the pillow, but commanding fingers clasped his chin, and the cup was presented once more.

"Do as I say. Cats claw and willow bark—for the pain."

Her Norse was strangely spoken, but he understood.

She fed him a thick broth, spoon by spoon, and although the sun shone bright through the open door, he wanted only to return to where the darkness wrapped him.

Each time he emerged from sleep, she was there—smoothing salve on his tender skin, changing the linens, making him drink or eat.

At last, the urge to sleep passed, and he was able to sit up.

The bed in the forge was not as he remembered it. More pillows had been added, and there was a sweet scent in the air. A jug of water was at hand, from which he took his fill.

He was enough himself to remember there had been a corpse. He sought out the place, but there was no evidence of it now—the stain had been covered over with fresh soil and branches of rosemary.

A moment later, Modwen knelt beside him.

"Better?" She lifted the edge of his dressing. "It's healing."

Warmth swelled his chest. Those silk-dark eyes, with only a hint of bruising now. He wasn't the only one healing.

My wife.

It wasn't necessary to name his feelings—only to accept them.

She touched his cheek. "Thank you." Her glance went to where his had rested, under the anvil. "It was my sin, but you took the blame."

"A husband protects his wife." He touched his hand to hers.

"You shouldn't have done it." She looked thoughtful, forlorn. "I told the jarl that it was me." Modwen stared at her lap. "He was angry."

"With you?" Magnus frowned.

"A little, but mostly with you—for being too brave, or foolish." She shrugged helplessly. "I don't know the word."

He wasn't sure he knew the word either, for whatever he'd been. There was something he'd had to prove, and it had taken a back full of lashes to do it.

"He said I was foolish, also, for thinking I was to blame."

Magnus nodded. "He's right. We're both foolish!"

She smiled at that.

"You still need to rest. Lie down."

"Only if you lie beside me." He shuffled to make room, and she did as he asked.

Her body fitted into his perfectly—the curve of her spine against his chest. The softness of her behind, too, where it was pleasing to him.

He brushed aside her hair, resting his head above hers, listening to her steady breathing as he surrendered to sleep. There would be no more bad dreams.

17

Suns and moons passed.

If he woke and Modwen was not there, he felt her absence keenly. Most times, she wasn't far. With the doors of the forge pulled wide, she set up her loom where he could see, and within distance of his call.

The hour of her lesson was the longest, during which he would wait for sign of her return. Afterwards, he coaxed her to sit with him and share her learning.

The children crept in, shyly at first, having been told by Modwen not to tire him with their chatter. From his ship chest he brought out a *Hnefatafl* set—made for playing on the long journey over, it had been a gift from his own sons. Taran inspected each wooden piece, carved with a peg beneath to fit into the board's holes.

Even in rougher weather, it hastened the passing of time.

Quickly, the two picked up the rules, and he soon left them to battle their wits without him.

The men came also to check on his recovery. Oft, they sat with him outside the forge, saying nothing of consequence but lifting his heart with their easy comradeship.

Father Godfrey had been summoned, so he'd heard, to judge the matter of Modwen's guilt. He decreed her free of sin, having acted in self-defence. Their god would forgive her. Magnus was glad of it, for he knew the torture of wrestling with one's fear. He'd spent years pleading for mercy from his own gods.

"Hasten the healing, brother, for you've a wife eagerly awaiting." Steinn winked. "Come Yuletide, I'd wager every bride's belly will be round and full, so we'll know if you've been slacking!"

Magnus said nothing, but the jest was not lost on him. The friends he'd known all his days were making lives anew. Was there time, yet, for him to do so?

Modwen had lost the man to whom she'd devoted her life, but she hadn't let grief rule her. She was generous-hearted, brave, and decent, and he wanted to bring ease to her life, protecting and caring for her.

Screwing his eyes tight, he cursed himself.

When would he be honest!

By the deadly fangs of Fenrir, he wanted more than that.

He wanted her physically, as any husband ought. What was holding him back? He'd thought it was a sense of duty to Solveig—an honouring of her memory—but that had been a lie.

With him unable to forgive himself, the depth of his self-blame had broken him. He'd been stumbling blindly, convinced he deserved only punishment. Those who'd murdered Solveig had taken a slice of his soul—but only because he'd allowed them to do so. Wherever she was now, he needed to believe she was at peace.

Before him was a second chance at happiness, and he wanted it. Badly. He wanted to banish the terrible loneliness. He wanted to look into the eyes of the woman he loved and know that she loved him in return. He wanted to show that love through the depth of his kisses and the warmth of his embrace.

He wanted, needed, yearned for Modwen.

He'd sent Alpia and Taran to join the others on the shore, collecting seaweed to be dug into the soil now cultivated on the headland. He wanted no interruptions. This time, he'd show Modwen what it meant to be loved by a Viking, and it would be no rushed affair.

He found her at her table, kneading dough to bake on the flat pan over the fire, her long braid hanging down her back, and wearing emerald green—several shades lighter than her eyes. Seeing him in the doorway, she paused in her work, seeming to tremble.

As he came to stand behind her, she didn't move.

He trailed his fingers down her arm, tracing the slender bend of her elbow, then continued slowly, until his touch was upon the pulse of her wrist. He lowered his mouth to her ear, and she tilted back her head to rest on his chest. He took her lobe between his teeth, tasting her, and his breath stirred the hair at the nape of her neck. She shivered. He brushed his lips to her throat, so lightly, inhaling the sweet scent of her skin.

His fingers made nimble work of the gown's fastenings on either shoulder, and he brought his arms round her, embracing her body through her thin shift. With his mouth buried in the crook of her neck, he pressed into her warmth, drawing her to him. She gave small whimpers at his caress—of her hips, her stomach, and her nip of her waist.

He cupped her breasts and groaned with need.

She was so beautiful, and she was his.

Modwen twisted, taking his lips with her own, and

he held her close. She curled her arms about his back, wanting to surrender herself to his kiss and to deepen it, sliding her tongue over his. Fierce and hungry, he left her breathless.

Snatching her up, he held her. An emotion more forceful than lust seemed to course through him, though just as reckless. The longer he drank her in, she felt his excitement grow, and warmth flooded her belly, knowing that he was ready to give himself to her again.

In a swift motion, he took her in his arms, carrying her to the bed. He laid her down, and her heart raced. She could not move, could not think. She knew only that she needed him to make love to her. She wanted to feel the length of his body against hers, and to be naked under the insistence of his mouth and hands.

He remained fully clothed, lifting her shift, then tossing it away altogether. His warrior hands, which worked daily with metal and weapons, were roughly calloused but now gently caressed, handling her with more tenderness than she could have imagined. He made free to explore every soft curve, leaving no part of her untouched. His kisses followed where his fingers roamed, grazing her thighs and belly, becoming more fervent.

When he enclosed her breast's tip, drawing hard, she felt it deep in her womb—a burning, aching need for all she knew he could give her. Low moans rose from her throat. His tongue teased her nipples, flicking gently before capturing them again. All the while, he clasped her to him, as if he would draw her into his own body entirely.

Still suckling, he reached downwards, stroking through her soft fur. His fingers slipped inside. Her sheath was tight, but he matched each caress with the pulling of his mouth, until she was all slickness, arching against the pressure of his hand. The pure ache of her desire pulsed beneath his fingertip.

When he drew away, he looked at her with an intensity that might once have scared her. Now, she held the mastery of his gaze, wishing him to see her as clearly as she saw him. She wanted to give herself fully, holding nothing back, yielding the softness of her body to his hardness, letting him dominate with his strength. Her fingers yearned to touch the contours of his chest and the rigid muscles of his abdomen.

With swift fingers, she unbuckled his belt, her knuckles brushing the solidity of his manhood. His cock sprang free, rising from the thatch of hair at his groin, and the tip glistened. He was harder than she'd ever seen a man, and thicker, and she wanted him inside her. She held her breath as he slid his hands beneath her thighs, raising her buttocks. Closing her eyes, she willed herself to relax, preparing for the penetration of his arousal.

But it was not his cock that plundered her sex. He was breathing deeply, inhaling her scent, pressing his lips to her fur. Briefly, she struggled, then gasped. He plunged deeply with his tongue, lapping at the source of her cream.

Dear God! Torture and Heaven all at once!

She curled her hips to one side, but he held her firmly to his mouth, hot and thorough.

"Oh!" she cried. "No!" Even as she wove her fingers into his hair, holding his head where she needed him, she whispered, "Don't stop!"

In return, he groaned, pulling her onto his devouring mouth.

His beard brushed between her legs—soft bristles against pale thighs and the lusciousness of her sex. *The smell of her! The taste!*

He drank her sweetness, stroking back and forth through silk and swollen arousal, seeking the tender bud. Her soft cries of pleasure were soon transformed to urgent need, driving him on, begging for him to take all that he wanted and more. Ravenously, he obliged, until his head swam, and she bucked beneath him, convulsing in quivering rapture.

She belonged to him, only to him.

As she rested replete, stretching languorously, he cast his garments to the floor, all the time watching. She loosened her dark curls from their braid, so that they fell soft over her shoulders and breasts. He rested his hands on her waist, appraising through half-closed eyes.

Trailing across his chest, she fingered his nipples, then raised her head to lick where she'd touched. She shifted her legs, offering herself, and his temptation was to thrust deep and bury himself within her warmth, but he resisted. He wished to give her a second storm of pleasure, and his release would be too swift if he entered her in such a fashion.

He reached beneath her body, squeezing her rump, and almost cast aside his resolve, lingering there, with her fullness filling his palm.

At last, he slipped his other arm under her back and brought her above him, so that she sat on his lap. With a laugh, she looked down, shaking her hair from her shoulders. She took the root of his erection and directed him to meet her sex, holding his gaze all the while, lowering onto his thickness.

She directed his hands to her breasts, and then rocked, stroking smooth against his shaft. She threw back her head, undulating, building her arousal, pressing his hands harder to her body.

He grasped her waist firm as she rose and fell, encouraging her to take him with greater vigour. Savagely, wildly, she rode him deep, her cries building until she rasped with joy. His own release came just as hot, in surging heat. Together, they burned, and he held on tightly, knowing he would never let her go.

They curled up together on the pallet, and he marvelled once more at her womanly perfection—the fullness of her hips and the softness of her skin. Her lips, swollen from his kisses, and her firm breasts, the tips tender from his attention. Between her thighs, his pleasure and her own, intermingled, and the thought of it made him wish to stir her and begin again.

18

He led her to the clifftops, looking beyond to where the sea was glimmering. He'd meant to speak first, but she found her words before he had the chance.

"If you want to return home, to your other life, to your sons, I understand." Swallowing, she bit her lip, keeping her gaze on the sinking sun.

They don't need me, he thought. *And what is there for me in Skalanes but memories I've never been able to bury?*

He wanted to live again.

He wanted Modwen.

To serve her all the ways a husband should. To redeem himself.

He'd give her not only the heat of his desire but the steadfastness of his warrior heart. He'd give her what she truly deserved.

By Thor and Odin, and all the gods, he'd worship her until her body became a part of his. He raised her fingers to his lips and placed a reverent kiss there, then pressed her hand, so soft, to his cheek.

She traced his scar, tilting back her head, and there was uncertainty in her expression. His fault, he knew. He wanted her to know all blame was his. She deserved to hear that, and to know the depth of feeling that grew within him. But how to make himself understood?

He cursed his lack of knowledge of her language. He'd never seen the need to learn more than a handful of words, and those long ago, in that time when he'd still had the heart to go a-Viking with the other men. He'd no choice but to speak Norse, hoping that she'd feel his meaning.

"My wife, long ago..." A band of iron seemed to encircle his chest, but he drew a deep breath, and then another. "She died."

Modwen squeezed his hand and gave the smallest of nods.

"The sadness inside—" He brought her palm to his chest, holding it there. He looked deeply into her eyes and saw everything a man could desire—her need for him, and her longing, her respect.

And the same look he'd seen in Solveig's eyes.

Love. It was love that had crept into his heart, even though he'd done all he could to shut it out.

"Can you forgive?" he asked. He bent his head

so his mouth hovered just above hers. His voice was hoarse. "I need you, wife."

"We need each other, husband."

And then she was unable to say anything more, for he lifted her off her feet, and his kiss—so tender—left no room for words.

There was a lifetime ahead, and so much yet to share. As the gods willed, their destiny would unfold, and they would face each day together.

EPILOGUE

The leaves shivered from oaks and birch, nights grew cold, and the animals of the forest sought refuge. All grew still in the woodlands, while Autumn mists swept the purple heather.

The turning season brought fierce winds driven in from the sea, and the folk of Achnaryrie sheltered in their homes. Fortunately, they'd harvested well, and none would lack for smoked meat nor fish. The grain stores would last, and each man had felled his share of timber to feed his winter fire.

Through the first snows, Magnus watched his wife's belly become high and round, her radiance blooming. Her hair grew thicker and more luscious, and her breasts larger than Magnus's hands could hold. He warmed her in their bed through the long, dark hours, finding time to learn one another's delights and comforts.

Magnus fired his furnace for the making of gifts, bestowing on Modwen a pair of brooches of his own design, intricately patterned, alongside a hair pin topped by a bird with outstretched wings. Taran had his own sword at last, and Alpia, a short dagger, the hilt worked with all the skills Magnus possessed.

Modwen had not been idle, weaving cloth of deepest green. Proudly, she presented matching tunics for Taran and Magnus, each embroidered with a pattern of ivy in a lighter shade. For Alpia, who was growing, there was a new undershift and gown, the yoke woven green and blue together. In their new finery, they would celebrate the turning of the year and give thanks.

Jul brought blizzards, as not seen in many years, but the Norsemen gathered in the jarl's hall for wrestling, riddles, and puns, for the singing of songs and telling of tales. Their drinking games brought much merriment, each man competing to devise the cleverest insults. Yet it was Gladys who proved the sharpest tongued, to her husband's amusement.

The fire pit blazed, filled with logs of oak and heaped high with fir branches and holly sprigs, over which roasted a boar brought down by Brandr's own arrow.

As dusk fell, they rolled out a giant wheel, carved from wood and set aflame, which Garth and Ragnar pushed off, to whirl across the headland—a burning symbol of the sun, cutting through the darkness, its path taking it over the cliffs and into the raging sea.

They stood and raised their cups in honour of those far away, and those who would drink with them no more.

Beneath swathes of mistletoe gathered from the forest by the hardiest of men, the warriors then shared with all the legend of Odin's Wild Hunt.

"He leads the souls of our ancestors, charging across the sky on Sleipnir, his eight-legged stallion," the jarl said, speaking soft to the children crouched at his knees. "None would dare look upon the *Ásgardr* riders, as the worlds of living and dead are not fast in these winter days."

"We'll leave gifts of food and drink in the snow," Rinda added swiftly. "So they'll pass on without danger, have no fear."

The Christian people of Achnaryrie gave their voices in marking their Saviour's day, but the story of winter darkness and the light that would come again was familiar, Modwen said, for hadn't such tales always been told, and wreaths of green hung to remind all of spring which would come.

In the months that followed, her growing child danced and kicked, though she often paused to sigh and catch her breath, rubbing the place where the babe moved. Modwen smiled at the life within her belly.

He'd been so young the first time that he'd paid

little mind to the changes in Solveig's body. Now, he marvelled at the wonder of it, getting close enough to Modwen's stomach to feel the babe's movements. He urged her to take her ease and let him fetch and carry whatever she needed.

With the softer breezes of late spring, Modwen's time arrived, and though her cries of pain froze Magnus's heart, fearful as he was for her safe delivery, their child was born quickly, aided by Myrna and Eithne.

A daughter!

With eyes as dark as his own and a head of lush hair.

He cried with joy at her delicate features.

As Modwen stayed abed, the babe snuggling at her breast, feeding lustily, Magnus sat beside her and wrapped both in his embrace.

How he loved them—this wife gifted to him by the gods, and this tiny child they'd created together. The feeling overwhelmed his heart.

Had he ever been this happy?

Yes, long ago—without thinking to be so again.

He cupped the child's head, pressing his lips first to Modwen's cheek, then his daughter's. She was frail now, but she'd grow strong like the other newborns, gifted as of late to his fellow warrior brothers and their brides.

The next generation of Achnaryrie was secure. The years would see these children grow, and there would be many more.

"She's all right, I suppose." Taran groaned. "But can we have a boy next time?"

"You must ask your mother that." Magnus ruffled the boy's hair. "For now, you have two sisters and must join me in their care and protection."

"A man knows his duty," Taran recited with a satisfied smile.

"He does." Magnus beckoned Alpia closer, giving her hand a squeeze, then placing it upon Taran's. "Now, off with you both, for the new planting has begun, and that's a job everyone must take part in."

Once they were alone, Magnus brought his lips to Modwen's and lingered there. For the time being, his wife's body—tempting as it was—belonged to the babe, but he would show his passion in his kiss. All the while, his daughter suckled heartily, her tiny mouth eager for the milk that would nourish her.

When Magnus broke off, his voice was rough. "I love you, wife."

"And I, you, dearest husband."

His thoughts turned to that first day they'd landed on the shore below the headland of Achnaryrie. Another lifetime, when he'd thought himself forsaken and believed his jarl's command to wed a cruelty wrought to torment him.

How little he'd known.

As if she were thinking the same, Modwen said, "I'm glad 'twas you."

She raised her chin in request of another kiss, and Magnus whispered softly in her ear, though there was no one else to hear his words or to disturb them. He murmured promises of love for Modwen, and when her lips touched his, Magnus knew the gods were smiling on him.

Explore the other romances within the VIKING SURRENDER series

Brandr - by Ashe Barker

Forced to wed a fierce Viking warlord to save her people, Eithne must surrender to her husband's stern discipline, yet his tenderness takes her breath away. A man of his word, Brandr vows to protect her village from its enemies.

But what of Eithne?

Who will protect her as she learns to care for this ferocious man who now leads her people and holds her heart in his mighty hands?

Ragnar - by Sky Purington

Intrigued by the symbol on his blade, Myrna chooses Ragnar for her husband. But how is she to love a man who lives in the past? Determined to remain faithful to his deceased wife, Ragnar both fights and craves Myrna, hungry for her healing touch. Will he give in and find sanctuary in her arms? Or will the shocking truth about his dagger end love before it begins?

Graeme - by Gianna Simone

Maimed and bitter, Graeme is forced to take a wife from the barbarians invading his shores. Resentful of her invading his solitary life, he vows to bend her to his will. Rinda grudgingly weds a man she barely knows—who hates her nearly as much as she despises him. Yet, despite their shared animosity, the wounded warrior and shield-maiden share an unexpected passion that soon consumes them both.

Magnus - by Emmanuelle de Maupassant

Magnus is tortured by memories of his wife's murder at the hands of savage berserkers, yet commanded to wed. The valiant warrior finds unexpected passion in his new bride's arms, but can Modwen's love heal the wounds of his battle-scarred heart—or will another's jealousy destroy them both?

Garth - by Sassa Daniels

A proud warrior, he hides a debilitating weakness. The village outcast, she's plagued by terrifying visions. Their marriage seems cursed from the start. But, as they come to terms with their union, will they find the love they both need?

Jerrik - by Felicity Brandon

Brigid: The last thing I need is a husband, especially some Viking brute commanding my surrender. Jerrik: Fight all you want, little Pict. You will yield to my desire...

Forced into a union she didn't seek, Brigid is terrified and aroused by Jerrik's masterful behaviour and carnal demands. But, when he saves her son from the ferocious ocean, Brigid realises he may be the hero she needs, as well as the man she craves.

Steinn - by Lily Harlem

Married to a barbaric beast, Gladys cannot believe her bad fortune. A rough and raw Norseman has taken to her home and her bed as if it's his right. But never fear, she has plans to do away with him, to rid him from her life...for good.

Steinn is thankful to the gods for his good luck. His new bride Gladys is a sexy little wild cat with curves and an ass to die for. Admittedly she needs a little training, and a fair bit of discipline, but he'll take her in hand if it's the last thing he does. Won't he?

Bjorn - by Jane Burrelli

A proud shield-maiden vowing never to be possessed by any man. A ruthless Viking warrior swearing to tame the bold beauty.
A battle of wills and consuming desire.
But who will conquer who?

Printed in Poland
by Amazon Fulfillment
Poland Sp. z o.o., Wrocław